14 DAY BOOK

This book may be kept
for 14 days only
It cannot be renewed

DIXON   Dixon, Stephen,
        1936-

        Long made short.

DATE DUE

LONG

MADE

SHORT

JOHNS HOPKINS: POETRY AND FICTION

John T. Irwin, General Editor

OTHER BOOKS BY STEPHEN DIXON

No Relief (stories), 1976

Work (novel), 1977

Too Late (novel), 1978

Quite Contrary (stories), 1979

Fourteen Stories (stories), 1980

Movies (stories), 1983

Time to Go (stories), 1984

Fall and Rise (novel), 1985

Garbage (novel), 1988

The Play (stories), 1989

Love and Will (stories), 1989

All Gone (stories), 1990

Friends (stories), 1990

Frog (novel), 1991

LONG
MADE
SHORT

STORIES BY

Stephen Dixon

The Johns Hopkins University Press

Baltimore and London

This book has been brought to publication with the generous assistance of the
G. Harry Pouder Fund.

The Johns Hopkins University Press
2715 North Charles Street
Baltimore, Maryland 21218-4319
The Johns Hopkins Press Ltd., London

Library of Congress Cataloging-in-Publication Data

Dixon, Stephen, 1936–
   Long made short / Stephen Dixon.
      p.   cm. — (Johns Hopkins, poetry and fiction)
   ISBN 0-8018-4738-9 (acid-free paper). — ISBN 0-8018-4739-7 (pbk. :
acid-free paper)
   I. Title.   II. Series.
PS3554.I92L66   1993
813'.54—dc20   93-11174

A catalog record for this book is available from the British Library.

Stories in this collection appeared in the following magazines, to which the
author and the publisher extend their thanks: "The Rare Muscovite" and
"Man, Woman, and Boy" in *Western Humanities Review;* "The Caller" in *Tri-
quarterly;* "Flying" in *North American Review;* "Crows" and "Battered Head" in
Boulevard; "Voices, Thoughts" in *Story Quarterly;* "Turning the Corner" in
Threepenny Review; "Lost" in *Yale Review;* "The Fall" in *Mississippi Review;*
"Moon" in *To* and *Partisan Review.* "The Rare Muscovite" also appeared in
Prize Stories, 1993: The O. Henry Awards (Doubleday / Anchor Books). "Man,
Woman, and Boy" also appeared in *The Best American Stories of 1993* (Houghton
Mifflin).

To Sergei Dovlatov

1941–1989

CONTENTS

The Rare Muscovite   1

The Caller   17

Flying   32

Man, Woman, and Boy   35

Crows   47

Voices, Thoughts   54

Battered Head   71

Turning the Corner   86

Lost   93

The Victor   100

The Fall   130

Moon   139

LONG
MADE
SHORT

THE
RARE
MUSCOVITE

I can be such an egotistical self-righteous pompous son of a bitch; unaccepting, nonaccepting, I can't think of the right word but it's what I so often am and all of it's what I was again. Moscow, my wife and I, she to research a book she's anthologizing and introducing, I just to accompany her and see a city and be in a country I've never been to, and it's really just the extra airfare, since restaurants are very cheap and the hotel room's the same for one or two. She—Marguerite—speaks Russian, will be working all day in libraries and with Russian contacts so, through a colleague in America weeks before we left, got an interpreter for me for the five weekdays. Svetlana shows up at our hotel at nine, half-hour before she's supposed to. I'm squatting in the little tub, reach over and push the door shut, and Marguerite lets her in. I overhear them: Good mornings in Russian, then "Please, if it's possible, everything in English from now on. I want to sharpen my interpreting facilities even better from your trip, and I'm planning of visiting America in a year. And my earliness—tardiness?—

earliness is because the metro got here faster than I thought and was less crowded than expected. Then our brave police downstairs let me up with a wave when I thought I'd have more difficulties. And I didn't want to walk around in the slippery cold or sit in the dreary lobby with everyone blowing smoke and sturgeon fumes on me and talking in their loud German and English and American voices, present employers—employees?—excluded of course. I had a stroke, you see, two years ago. Recovered from this side being paralyzed to where I could barely walk. Twelve almonds a day, a healer from Kiev said—the doctors could offer no medicine but time for me. You might think it madness, I know so much how Americans rely on science, but the almonds worked, I'm sure of it, and I don't want to get excited. I can't afford to, you say?—by having to tell them off to their faces, all those bloated businessmen elephants blowing loud smoke and talk on me. I am one of those rare Muscovites who—whom? Let me get it correct now, *who*. Who detests those burning props."

I get dressed in the bathroom, come out, introduce myself, make coffee for us, take out sugar packets and coffee cake and tiny Edam cheeses we got on the plane with our dinner and snack, offer her peanut butter and dried salami and crackers we brought with us. "You don't get anything like this here," she says, "unless you wait on line for hours or buy it in the dollar stores, which I'll take you to," she says to me. "Hams in tins, coffee in cans, the best sardines and cheeses and most overpriced caviar. You won't need those perhaps, for only a week's visit in a hotel. But if you have Russian friends who do or you want to make a gift out of to them, that's also what they have there. And lemon and peppered vodka and Scottish scotch and Ararat, you know what that is?" "Da," I say. "Ah, listen, wonderful—possible he doesn't need an interpreter. But people say it can be as good or as better as the best French cognac. I wouldn't know since I'm also rare in Moscow in that I've never had a taste for alcohol. Maybe for my bad tooth, as a girl, but nothing else. And also at the Beriozka American cigarettes to kill people is what you get there too. One carton of them, none other than Marlboros, would be equivalent to, at black market rubles for dollars, a month's wages for the average worker here, or fifty rubles less. If you want to, we'll go. For if you return to America and your wife tells Millie you didn't have an opportunity to buy the best Russian whiskies and gifts, because I was taking you to all the more cultural places, I shall be very embarrassed and dismayed."

"No no," I say. "Any place you take me to is fine, since it'll all be new to me. Though if we want Ararat and vodka, better I hear at the duty-free store at the airport going home."

"But for use in your room? Marguerite tells me she'll be entertaining scholars here. Perhaps you brought the much preferred American whiskey with you. Or you don't drink or once did but went A.A., which is only beginning here. It's not that? If it was, or should it be 'were'?" He throws up his hands, points to Marguerite and says "She knows." "Oh, small difference, since we both know what I meant, and I have the few places and hours the A.A. clubs meet each week. Anyway, it's all up to you. I am simply here to coast you through. And the truth of the matter is that the Beriozkas, though something to see for their glamorous contradictions if not outright falsehoods to the rest of Moscow and present Russian life, have no real appeal to me."

But what am I getting at with all this? I had an idea of saying right at the start "Happens again," and then explaining what does. She gets a stroke our third weekday here, dies, and I didn't especially care for her almost from the moment I heard her through the bathroom door—actually got irritated, but not visibly, by her almost incessant talking and parading of her knowledge and vast learning. She seemed to know something or a lot about everything we spoke about or saw. She was familiar with the details of Marguerite's project and doctoral dissertation and knew the works of the people Marguerite was going to see, as well as every writer, painter and composer I mentioned and building we visited or I pointed out. Knew the dates, history, influences, inner meanings, could quote lines, cite pages and recite poems and so on—I, what? I forget what I started out saying. But she has this stroke, dies, police have to break down her apartment door to get her two days after her stroke and I feel very bad about it of course and guilty I bad-mouthed her so much to Marguerite and asked her to phone her to call her off after the second day, at least for a day and then I'd see how I felt. "I want to walk around alone, not meet any schedules, get lost on the metro if I want with only the few Russian words I know. Find a farmers' market by myself and the Tolstoi museum and Tolstoi's house again if I like, which I think I would but without her telling me who painted what picture on the wall and who the people are in the portraits and what famous composer played what famous composition on the grand piano there. I just want to feel the place, guess which side of the bed Tolstoi slept, and those desks of his and Sofia's and no electric lights and that sad room behind theirs where their youngest son—I forget his name, though she told me, and I think he was the youngest— died of scarlet fever in that oversized crib she said was a typical seven year old's bed then, or maybe he died in the hospital and she said he only got sick at home. For sure she had it right, whatever she told me. Or just to stay in our room finishing *War and Peace* and maybe going downstairs to the hotel café for a coffee and bun." And I feel if I had let her continue being my interpreter and guide, though we never used that word, instead of giving her a paid day off—paid, it's so absurd, since it was so little money and because she has no survivors we now don't know whom to send it to—she might have somehow survived, or at worst been with me when she had the stroke and I could have got help for her and saved her life. Or been with us, if we again took her to the hotel restaurant for dinner that night—and why not? since she knew which foods were freshest, so was an asset of sorts, and she didn't ask for more wages and the dinner was certainly cheap enough. But she died in her room that Wednesday, might not have had anywhere to go except to stand in the cold for hours on different food lines—she was retired but not even sixty. And maybe was in-censed at me—knew I didn't like her much for not very good rea-sons but stayed because she needed the money—or worried the job wouldn't work out because of what she sensed I felt about her, or grieved or got angry over it or both or something else and that somehow provoked the stroke. But I feel partly responsible for it, also that I wasn't there when I possibly could have been to help her when she got the stroke. And when I say "happens again" I mean because I've done things like that before. Bad-mouthed people for inadequate reasons—there probably aren't any good ones—just to avoid seeing them that night, for example, because they were preventing me from doing something I thought I might want to— just their presence would—or they had achieved some sort of stat-ure or success that let's say I secretly wanted, which I'm not saying she did though I have to admit I admired her intelligence tremendously, and though nothing so bad as a stroke or anything near it happened to any of them I always knew I was wrong in this attitude and regretted it and told myself I wouldn't do it again and sometimes only told myself I should try my hardest not to.

I didn't say what I really wanted to there, only because for whatever it is—my inability to say things clearly and straight and because I really don't have the means to—the language, words, I'm simply unable to do it well, on paper and orally most of the time also, besides not probably having the necessary kind of intelligence and insights. I don't even know if what I just said makes much sense, but let me get on with this. I was where before? Where was I? I'm trying to convey another person and, without being explicit, a person's feelings about her death and the way it changes ordinary life when it suddenly comes and what it can bring out in himself. That and more. Anyway, first place she takes me to that first day—Monday—is Red Square. "*Krasnaya*—'red'—I'd also like to teach you Russian words connected to the places we go to, which is the easiest way to learn them—through practical identification. Like *ulitsa*—'street'—which you'll see everywhere after a word like Herzen or Gorki on buildings and street-post signs, but first I must also teach you the Russian alphabet. And we might as well get Krasnaya Ploschad out of the way—see what I mean now? You understood without questioning me. But you can't be allowed to return home without saying you've been there, can you?"

"I think I can. But okay. Even though Marguerite and I went there the Saturday we got here—she insisted I see it at night—I never saw it in the day and nothing was open."

"Shall we walk? It's only two kilometers or and a half, and I can walk that far. It's supposed to be healthy for me besides." I ask how the sidewalks are—"It looks cold and wet out"—and she says icy and I suggest we take the metro or a cab. I didn't want her falling or holding on to me for so long a walk. "If you have dollars to pay or packs of American cigarettes to show and give away we can get a cab, something most Muscovites can't do here. I doubt you'll want to see inside the Kremlin buildings. They're rather vulgar—glittery jewels and gold and thrones—though you might want to see the domes over the Kremlin. But Saint Basil's in Krasnaya Ploschad has some of the best of those and later today or tomorrow we'll go to Novodevichy—*novo*, which is one of the forms of 'new'—which I think has the city's most beautiful of them. And I'd like taking you by train to Novgorod, which to me has the world's most beautiful of all."

She goes on like that. Steers me where she wants to go, doesn't think much of my suggestions. Arabat Street, where I'd like to get my gift buying done with: *matryoska* or *maritroska* dolls—I can never seem to get the word right—and painted wooden boxes and barrettes and decorated potholders and things like that. "Exclusively for tourists," she says, "who want their pockets combed through and gypsy beggar boys to steal their wallets and socks and shoes. Oh, they'll do it, and with baby brothers on their backs to distract you. But if you insist to go there, I won't stop you, but it's walk walk walk through unruly crowds for practically one of your miles." Chekhov Museum—"Ugly, not at all brings to vivid life the personality and living style of the man. But you love him, is that why? He's not Tolstoi, but I like his work very much too. 'Toska'—that's 'misery' or 'grief' or really 'long drawn-out sorrow'—not translatable as one word, and you can always remember it by the opera of the same name. A touching story. Very few as good except 'Ivan Ilyich,' which is more than touching—it's terrifying. This man reconciling himself to death after such an empty, trivial—how should I say it?—unenlightened life? I read it once a year. Just as your *War and Peace* there I try to every three years or anytime I need some tranquillity of spirit and mind. You were right to bring only that book with you—it serves the place of an entire library. Unfortunately there is little left of the Russian soul that's in that novel." The most grandiose metro stations— "For tour buses to empty themselves out into only, except for regular riders like myself who truly use it. You'll be staring up at the statuary and chandeliers while getting bumped by our rudest inhabitants, too ignorant or impolite or perhaps too eager in a rush to excuse themselves, even to foreigners. But you wish to see these stations—and the deepest you say, for some unexplained reasons?—then we'll go to these too."

After we all have dinner at the hotel restaurant and Svetlana leaves I say to Marguerite "Did you see the way she made those last-minute sandwiches? I mean, she got a free meal—I'm not begrudging her it, since it was cheap enough and she wasn't too intrusive at the table and I had enough wine in me to ward her off when she was. And I know there's a shortage of dairy stuff in Moscow. But Jesus, have some self-respect and maybe consideration for us, since this is our hotel, and don't stuff the rest of the table bread into your bag and fill the two slices of bread left on your plate with a quarter pound of butter and wrap that up for home too. I shouldn't be saying all this, right? since I probably don't know what I'm talking about."

"It's that you forget. She asked our permission first. She's giving the butter to an old woman in her building who can't get any and the bread I guess she figures the woman will like also or else just that the kitchen will throw it away. But suppose she was drying the bread for herself and hoarding the butter for a day when she won't have any, like tomorrow perhaps? So what."

"Okay, fair. But also, when she talks to us I kind of get upset"— "You get very upset"—"I get a little less than that upset that she keeps me out entirely, and it's in English. When I do say something when you're around she often looks at me as if I were a kid who's barged in when he's been warned not to, as if this is adult conversation only so buzz off. You're the big genius and intellectual toiler she's saying—after all, it's your project we've come here for. I'm just a stupid site-gazer—didn't know Red Square wasn't inside the Kremlin—but at least I was honest enough to admit it. Doesn't know the difference between the Tver—that the way to say it?—and Novgorod Russian icon schools. Why should I know? Who does but an art expert of that period or field or someone who has few books to choose from in libraries and stores but all the time in the world to read? But credit me with a little intelligence and conversational interest or skills or whatever you want to call it. Someone who can on occasion talk with some knowledge and depth about the less poppy and mundane things. For instance, also credit me with—but nothing, when at the Pushkin, seeing me standing there staring at the Van Goghs for a few minutes, she asks me do I like them. 'You bet,' I said, which is what I usually say in front of Van Goghs, for what am I going to do when I'm still in a state of enthrallment, go into every crack, dab, dot and corner? But she gives me the French expression about each to his own taste or gut and then starts in with this pro-Monet and -Cézanne and anti-Vincent treatiselike argument or lecture I could hardly understand it was so over my head, or else she didn't know how to deliver it clearly and succinctly in English. But how these three Van Goghs all on the same wall are critically puffed up by unscrupulous experts, dealers and museums so people—like me, I'm sure she's saying—who know little to zero about art and artistry will pay fifty million bucks apiece for. My point is she thinks I'm uncultured, or barely cultured—certainly not intelligent. A walking talking absurdity when you think this shmuck also teaches at a university. Even if it were phys ed or home ec I taught—still, he represents the academy so should be much smarter, know several languages backwards, be able to communicate without hesitation and with full intellectual rigor and appropriate ornate words what he knows, sees and likes instead of being someone who probably always needs a thesaurus when he writes and talks. The typical example of the stereotyped American tourist she's shown around Moscow or just interpreted for before. Except of course you—ah, the intelligentsia. And those rare nonacademic people like the ones in Boston who gave you her name—fancy journalists, magazines—but so cultivated she kept telling me: educated, eloquent, polyglottal—at least the guy—worldly and well read and with even an executed Decembrist count way back in his family. Because I've no advanced degrees or easy time with the spoken language and have little political feeling or at least nothing much to say about it for either of our countries, she thinks I've no mind of my own and so have to have everything explained."

"It can't be all that bad and she has a wonderful itinerary for you tomorrow. The Tolstoi Museum, a farmers' market or two where you can get me some cracked walnuts and real Russian honey and anything that looks unusual there as gifts and will travel well for home. And the Andronikov monastery"—"Great, more icons"—"Don't go if you don't want, but also for its ancient tiny church and onion domes. And the G.U.M. department store to buy records for a quarter and a znachki shop there with the largest selection of them in the city. To impress her, pronounce the store 'Goom.' " "Goom, Goom." "Then step in with her someplace, get a taste of a workers' restaurant or café—she knows it all, and maybe over food alone you'll get to know and appreciate each other better. Anyway, she'll show you the ropes, how to use the trolley and pay phone and to shop without being cheated and show your dollars without getting mugged. By the time she's through with you, you'll be exhausted but have a map of the city in your head. Then you have a day off and she from you. It's for me too you'll be doing this. I'll be too busy to go shopping even one afternoon. And though I've seen most of it before you can tell me what you saw and also take pictures to show me and the kids later on."

Svetlana shows up on the dot next morning. We see things by foot, trolley, metro, occasional cab for a five-dollar bill Marguerite was told to bring about twenty of to Moscow for just something like this. Svetlana says once "Am I talking too much?" She is but I say "Nope." "I've tendencies towards talk, possibly for being sequestered in my slight space the rest of the days and the one woman I see most to take care of doesn't say three words a time. But I'm an honest person, you're visiting a culture where honest persons with words is almost a belief, so you want to be an honest person too, don't you? Tell me to my face if I'm twisting your ears as the English like to say, and perhaps the Americans too, or showing you too many things too fast to digest." "No no, I mean it, everything couldn't be better, thanks."

I don't want to be with her for lunch so I say I think I'm still suffering from jet lag and would like a nap at my hotel, would she mind eating alone? I give her money for the first-floor café, go upstairs and lie on my bed and drink coffee and read, she rings from the lobby an hour later. More places and constant information and chatter. "Are you sure I'm not talking too much?" "Why, do you think you are?" "Well, I might be." "No, absolutely not, it's all fine." Every monument and theater and famous person's birth or living place and also every building we pass by foot, trolley and cab that looks interesting architecturally or stands out because of its size she has something to say about. "That so? Yes, hmm, so this is where it is, I didn't know that."

We meet Marguerite for dinner at a Georgian restaurant she had to make reservations for two days ago, and in the cab back to our hotel we drop Svetlana off at a metro station. She hands us each several candies. "Special, hard to get because individually wrapped and the ingredients very select. They're made by an acquaintance of mine in the Kremlin's confectionary kitchen and often given in droves to dignitaries and diplomats. We ought to export them simply for their colorful wrappers. Bears and squirrels—children would love them." "That's very kind, thank you," I say. "I don't eat candy myself but will definitely try one, though not now because I'm too full, and save the rest for my girls." Marguerite's told her tomorrow will be a paid day off and asks if she'd like the first three days' pay now. "All at once, please. I wouldn't want to ride the metro with it. Too much in dollars and one of our now many clever Moscow thieves might see it on my face." "And on the fifth day?" I say. "Will he see it on my face you mean? No, since that day I'll hire a taxicab or continue with yours, flush like an American tourist or spending as freely as one. But because I'm Russian, all for the sum or extra one of a dollar, and then hide the money in my room for one of your rainy days. That is yours?" "Ours and probably the English's too."

Later I say to Marguerite "Know why she wants all her wages at once?" "Something disparaging, I suppose." "No, just conjecture born out of insight or something. Because she thinks we'll have to give her a bigger tip for the whole fifty than if we only gave her her last day's pay on Friday. She's a shrewdie all right, and even shrewder how well she disguises it." "Disguises what?" "Everything. Or just things—some. Holding back—being extra gracious to me when we're alone when I know damn well what she thinks of me intellectually, or maybe just culturally—we've spoken of it. And this not wanting her pay day by day because of the increment, the incremental—because with more . . . well, you know—or maybe I'm being far-fetched on this. But other things." "That's what I'm asking, what? Did she ever do or say anything in particular to make you question her motives this way?" "As I said, just little things I've picked up but nothing right now, other than what I've mentioned, that comes to mind." "Well I think you're way way off about her. She's a touch sad but decent, and energetic and enthusiastic. And I only wish I had the time to be taken around by such a knowledgeable person who knows the city so well, even if she is so garrulous, and you were the one doing the bookwork all day. Actually, I think you'd like that more." "No, I'm enjoying my rest away from work. And true, I suppose I should feel lucky having her for so little money. But the greater truth is I feel luckier being on my own tomorrow. Anyway, not to change the subject, I was thinking just now: '*da, da*'—what a nice soft way to say yes."

But to move along. She doesn't call Wednesday morning as she said she would to find out what time she should come Thursday morning. Marguerite calls her and she doesn't answer. She doesn't call Thursday morning. Marguerite calls her every fifteen minutes, thinking maybe she was out all night, slept at a friend's—has a secret life she never gave us a clue about, she says—or got in after midnight last night, when Marguerite stopped calling, and didn't call us after that because she felt it was too late, and was up and out for groceries or something early this morning. We leave the phone off the hook—each room has its own number, so it's all direct—when we go to the hotel restaurant for our complimentary breakfast. Marguerite calls when we get back, then asks me to stick around an hour more before going out on my own if that's what I plan to do. "When she was outside she might have had trouble getting a pay phone or misplaced our number or didn't have the two kopecks on her and nobody could give her change—anything, and she just got hold of a phone. If you want, which you probably won't, call every fifteen minutes or so—she might have just got home. But I'm a little worried about her, aren't you?" and I say "Of course, it doesn't seem like her, but I'm sure it's nothing," and she leaves for her appointment. I wait but don't call, figuring if she just got home first thing she'd do would be to call. I leave after an hour, walk around the old section of the city, try to find some buildings in *War and Peace* Marguerite said are still supposed to be here—the Rostovs' mansion, Pierre's house—but can't find the streets, even though they're on my map, and no one, if they're hearing me right and understanding the few Russian words Marguerite taught me yesterday to make myself understood in something like this, seems to have heard of them; stop in a café for "*odin kofe, mineralenaya voda* and *dva bulka*"—woman shakes her head—"*bulki, bulka,* two," holding up two fingers and then pointing to some rolls on the counter behind her, "*mais*—but not sweet ones, *nyet sakhar, pzhalesta,*" and she gives me mineral water and coffee without the lump of sugar that usually comes with it and takes enough change out of my palm to pay for it while I'm trying to find in it what amount I think she said.

Marguerite calls Svetlana before we go to the hotel restaurant for dinner, calls when we get back to our room. "I'm really worried now," she says, "I know something's wrong. We know she isn't the type to promise to come—to say she'll call the night before to see precisely what hour we want her—and then just to disappear.

And with that stroke she had two years ago—" "Oh yeah, that's right, the stroke, I forgot. So what do we do?" She calls a scholar she met the other day who said he knows of Svetlana but he only has her phone number, not her address, and doesn't know anyone who does; but he'll make some calls. "Even if we had her address," I say, "what would we do with it? She told me it's about an hour's metro ride to her stop—lots of changes and at the end of the line. Or a couple of changes, but anyway, 'couple' meaning what to her—two, three, four? We'd go out there at this hour when people all over the city are getting bumped on the head and robbed? Even by cab—or of course by cab if we could get one or one would take us that far—we'd be sure he'd wait? If he didn't we'd be screwed." "Not that. But say we found someone who knows her and lives near her? Or someone who doesn't but as a favor to us might want to help her. Maybe that person could phone a friend and go over— two men. Or just you and him. What I'm saying is Russians still do that, put themselves out for strangers, especially one intellectual for another. And if this person didn't want to do it but lived fairly close to her, which would mean you wouldn't go because he couldn't come in for you and then go back there and so on, I'd say we'd pay the fare—cab, anything. And would a carton of Marl-boros—a few weeks' salary for some at the regular exchange— encourage a friend of his to go along with him? Meaning, would it encourage *him*? But I've seen the way they've helped me. With leads, contacts, books, unpublished papers and notes and tapes very few American scholars would let me see and hear and copy down. And accompanying me clear across town for something and then waiting there while I worked or saw someone so they could take me back here."

She calls several people she's met, and through them friends and colleagues of theirs, but the one person who's heard of Svetlana doesn't even know her phone number. The first scholar she spoke to calls back and says nobody he contacted knows where she lives or how to find out. "I give up for now," she says. "Maybe she's okay and off doing something we haven't thought of yet, but I seriously doubt it." "I hope we're wrong," I say. "You mean you think it's no good too?" "Looks it. But as you said, we've only just met her so there's lots we don't know."

Little past midnight, we just got into our beds and shut the night table lights, the phone rings. A woman says "Abel, yes?

Hello, I'm Katya Sergeyeva, very good friend of Svetlana. Pardon me for upsetting you if this is nothing, but I'm extremely worried for her. Was she with you all of today?" "Let me put my wife on please. This is very important so if there's any language problem, she can speak Russian." She tells Marguerite she and Svetlana have spoken every day with each other since Svetlana's stroke. Yesterday she thought Svetlana went with us someplace outside of Moscow and got back late or stayed overnight at a hotel with us there. Now that she knows we haven't seen her for two days she's sure something's wrong. She's going to go over to her apartment now with a friend. If Svetlana doesn't answer she'll get the police to break down the door. Marguerite tells her we'll do whatever we can to help so please count on us and call anytime tonight, no matter how late. We read for a few minutes, then she yawns and hearing it I yawn right after and we agree we should try to nap. I wake up once thinking maybe Katya called but we didn't hear it in our sleep, though the phone only rings loudly, and cover Marguerite up and turn off the lights.

Katya calls just when Marguerite's about to dial her. She didn't get back to us last night because it was very late and things were still so unresolved. They got to the apartment, knocked, nobody answered and they didn't hear anything behind the door so they called the police who said they couldn't get there till ten this morning. "They couldn't get there?" I say when Marguerite translates it for me while still on the phone. "What if she still has some breath this minute but dies a few seconds before they get there?" "Shh," she says, signaling she can't hear what Katya's saying. Katya says she and several friends are going to meet the police now at Svetlana's and she'll call soon as she has some news, but she's convinced now Svetlana's dead. She also told Marguerite that after they knocked and called through the door last night they went to about twenty apartments in the building and nobody had seen Svetlana for two days. "They went around asking at one and two in the morning?" "I told you, people here do that. Not the police, as you heard, but you can call on your friends and most of your neighbors anytime." "So why didn't they all get together last night and knock down the door? Police wouldn't come, hell with them, or is it it's really maybe some highly penalizable crime?" "Possibly. Probably."

Phone rings two hours later. Marguerite stayed around long as she could but then had to leave for an important appointment that couldn't be rescheduled. "Abel, yes? Katya here, most unexpected news," and then her voice cracks and she speaks excitably in Russian. "Speak English, please, I understand very little Russian. *Nye govoryu po russki, nye govoryu po russki,*" and she says "*Nyet, nyet,* not okay, can't. Wait." A woman gets on and says "Hello, I am Bella, good friend of Katya and Svetlana. It is terrible to speak to you, sir, only this once with only this terrible news for you. I speak English not good but try. Svetlana is dead. She has stroke Wednesday, your day, she must have, we and police today believe, that made her that way, killed her. Great pity. Much sorrow. Wonderful woman. Intelligent and kind and so nice to this building and people and everywhere she goes. It is very very sad." "Very. I'm terribly sorry. Please tell Katya that. And what is her phone—telephone number, please, even though I think my wife took it. But what is it if she didn't take it so she can phone Katya later," and she gives me it.

For a couple of days after I think how I would have liked it to turn out. I wouldn't show any signs I disliked her, was annoyed or irritated by her. If I did and it was evident to her I'd quickly apologize, saying it was something in me, personal, being away from my work maybe, maybe worried about my kids, too much of that good lemon vodka last night or bad sturgeon, other excuses, but nothing she'd done. If she apologized for being such a chatterbox, as she said of herself once, covering her mouth with her hand, I'd say "Great, chatter away, don't hold back for my sake, because most of what you're saying is interesting and new to me, and better someone who talks and makes sense than keeps sullen and still." We'd go here, there, lunch, dinner with Marguerite, stop for coffee, tea for her, *bulki, torte* or whatever the plural for them, which I'd ask her for, I'd suggest she take me inside the Kremlin, the Tolstoi and Chekhov museums, whatever church and monastery she wants me to see in the city and outside it. At lunch I'd give her some of the plastic sandwich bags I brought from New York and would say "Butter all the bread you want and stick them in the bags and the bags into your pocketbook. Less messy, and the food's only going to go to waste or be taken home by the kitchen staff. I'd take some myself but we do all that kind of buttering and cheese-taking and other secret hoarding at the hotel's breakfast buffet every day." Children's toy store, Pushkin museum again, where I might say maybe she has a point about the Van Goghs and I've been duped as much as the next guy about his work, since I'm no art expert, exhibition hall of contemporary Russian painting she spoke about and I'd wanted to see but begged off because I didn't want her lecturing me. I'd take her up on teaching me ten Russian words and a couple of phrases and one complete sentence a day and testing me occasionally on the Russian alphabet till I could read or at least sound out all the stores' names and street signs. We'd talk about books and stories we've read, plays we've seen, she here, I in the States. Farewell dinner at a Czech restaurant Marguerite and I had talked weeks ago about ending our trip with. We'd toast to one another, to good literature, to Tolstoi and Chekhov and Babel, Ahkmatova and Tsvetaieva and the endurance of all great art, to the success of Marguerite's project, to my work at home, to Svetlana and everything she does and for being such a fine interpreter and companion and friend and showing and teaching me things I never would have seen or known, to our two girls and all our families and friends, to returning to Moscow soon, to her visiting America and our being her sponsors and me her guide for a day or two, to continuing good relations between our countries, democracy in hers, to eternal peace between them, peace and disarmament everywhere and good health and happiness and cooperation everywhere too and more dinners for the three of us like this one, future toasts. Then we'd ask the restaurant to order a taxi and we'd drop her off at a metro station, kiss each other's cheeks, give her her five days' salary and a twenty-dollar tip and some kind of present—one of the scarves Marguerite brought as presents from America, cologne from America or probably both if she hasn't given them away yet. Or I'd get out of the cab and help her out and then kiss her, or we'd drive her home no matter how far out of the way and wait in the cab till she got in her building. Or I'd walk her to her first-floor hallway and stay there till she was upstairs and in her apartment or had enough time to get inside. Or we'd cab straight to our hotel and give our presents and enough extra fare in dollars for the cab to take her home.

Back in New York Marguerite says "It's so strange to think the last day you see some person, very active and energetic and seemingly healthy, is the last day of that person's life, or the last night." "Very odd," I say, "very." "And I forgot to tell you. That Katya—you remember her, Svetlana's friend who went over there with the police? Well she said Svetlana was planning to give us a little party at her place after her last workday, or really not so little. After dinner, that she would invite some of her friends— interpreters and people in teaching and editing—and ask me for names of people I'd seen who might want to come, or anyone I wanted. I doubt many of them would have come, unless they lived close by. And I would have done what I could, without hurting her in any way, to dissuade her. But that's something for her to want to do, since she was short of money and you'd think she'd be too tired that day to give it. I'm thinking now though. I'm having this very bad thought, without wanting to sound as if I don't appreciate what she wanted to do, but that her stroke saved us from it. It would have been the last thing I wanted, at her place or any place but, to be honest, less at her place. Her friends were probably bright and nice but a bit dull. Or maybe not, but you know, I just wouldn't see the reason for the party. I don't know how we could have refused it though, do you?" "Too tired and busy. We were leaving in a day and a half and you needed to see some more people or do research or go over your notes or something. And we also had to pack and were almost too tired for even that."

THE
CALLER

My wife answers and says "It's for you," and hands me the cordless and I go into the kitchen with it because she's working in the living room and shut the door and say hello and a woman says "Jack, hi, it's Ramona Bauer," and I shout "What, Ramona Bauer?—not my old friend Ramona," and she says "That's right, and my old friend Jack, how are you?" and I say "God, how are you, I'm fine, but how are you and what have you been doing?" and she says she's still in New Haven, different house though, and has two children, girl in college, boy graduating high school, girl has been a delight her entire life and at the very top of her class since kindergarten and is already a fantastic scientist, boy has some emotional problems but nothing that won't be solved, she and her husband are divorcing after being married close to nineteen years and together for twenty-two, and I say "Sorry to hear that, it must be a very difficult thing to go through, especially for the children," and she says "Not as much as it's been for everyone enduring the two of us living together the last five years, and if you're saying part of my son's problem is because of the breakup, that's true but a small part of it and will also be worked out," and I say "Well good, I'm glad. I remember your husband. He has an unusual Slavic name I could never pronounce or spell," and she says "Kaczmarek," and I say "Kaczmarek, I still wouldn't know how to spell it without seeing it, but he liked to climb mountains and jump from airplanes, and was a radio producer or assistant to one last time I saw you, which was when I drove to New Haven when you were living together," and she says "Now he's a TV and movie producer—documentaries mostly," and I say "Good for him. I also read the obituary of your mother and sent you a note about it through their old address," and she says "You did? I never got it though my father was still living there till about five years ago," and I say "He's all right, I hope," and she says "Ninety-one and still, last I heard, never a health problem and barely a checkup, knock wood," and she raps something twice, and I say "Anyway, I sent the note," though now I remember I wanted to and maybe even wrote it but never sent it out, and she says "If he got it he never told me—did you address it directly to me?" and I say "Yes, with probably something about my condolences to your whole family," and she says "That was sweet of you—believe me, if I'd received it I would have replied," and I say "That's okay, it happens. How is your brother, by the way— still in films? Because I haven't seen his name on one for it must be fifteen years, but then there's few American films I go to though I think I would have caught his name in the ads if he had any billing," and she says "Listen, less we say about him or any of my family, the better. I've sort of cut myself off from all of them, even my father—imagine," and she laughs, "their little pip-squeak Ramona, the one who could always be bossed around and whom they treated as if she never and could never grow up. Well, they still treat me that way and I'm fifty-three, so I just said—this was in relation to my divorce when I told them—'Fuck you, gang,' and I don't hear from them anymore, not even my oldest and closest sister and certainly not my wacko brother," and I say "She—but you don't want to talk about it," and she says "No, what?" and I say "The oldest one, Denise or Diana, lived in Mount Kisco, didn't she?" and she says "What a memory you have about things I like to forget. Dina still does—Ms. Stability—hasn't moved or been upset by anything in forty years," and I say "On Elderberry Street, number one-o-four or six," and she says "Eight, but still, that's fantastic and you even got the berries right this time," and I say "I didn't use to?" and she says "I don't know, didn't you? For I was only kidding, but what about your family—your mother?" and I say "She's old and ailing and not altogether there sometimes—her memory of what you just tell her goes pretty quickly but she's still good with the distant past—she's living in the same apartment where you first knew me, though with a full-time companion," and she says "What a dear woman—I'm sorry she's not well—please mention we spoke and give her an extra big hug from me next time you see her," and I say "Will do," and she says "I'm serious—tell her I still think of her fondly and give her that hug," and I say "I'll probably see her later today—I do almost every day for at least an hour, so I'll do what you say," and I will tell her though more likely tomorrow but won't give the hug—it would seem too silly: "Here's a hug from Ramona Bauer, woman I was engaged to almost thirty years ago, remember her?" and passing on kisses and hugs even to my own children isn't something I like to do, and she says "What about the rest of your family—your brothers and sisters, they all well?" and I tell her one died in a bicycle accident twelve years ago last week, one's a fully recovered alcoholic now a social worker in alcohol abuse, another moved to Texas to open a macrobiotic restaurant and we hardly hear from her anymore, the fourth has been married four times in the last twelve years and has seven children and now seems to have taken up with the future number five—"I don't know what she's got but it's something that hasn't slackened," and she says "Wow, some rundown and such woe, and your father?—because you didn't mention him," and I say "Yes, seventeen—no, eighteen years ago this January," and she says "I'm sorry, but I'm glad your mom's still around—she was a doll, treated me wonderfully, comfortably, one of the family." "And my father didn't, I know—well, mixed marriage and all, which we almost had with almost mixed children. Not that it meant anything to us but he sure wasn't keen on it—he was from a very religious family and was observant himself till just a year before I was born when both his parents died," and she says "I understand, I'm not saying that—anyway, all in the past," and I say "Right, in the past, but you have to know that much as he protested, you won him over without even trying," and she says "Oh, I tried all right—that guy was tough to crack." "What I meant was your high spirits, brains, good looks and humor and stuff and that you were an acting success so fast," and she says "Oh yeah, a big big success," and she laughs and I say "What's funny?" and she says "Nothing, or success—just nothing," and I say "Okay . . . and how's Leonard What's-his-name—Stimmell, because I've a funny story about him," and she says "Good ole Lenny, one of my other dearest old friends—I see him whenever I come to town, practically—he's such a gas, and talk about spirit? Nothing's gonna stop him but everything will," and I say "You mean he's still plugging away at acting without much success?" and she says "Thirty-plus years of the best bit roles in TV commercials and walk-ons in soaps and occasionally small to fairly good roles in hole-in-the-wall theaters and summer stock, and same wife, no kids—they'd interfere with his constant auditions and he said they also couldn't afford them, Laurie still doing temporary office work while pursuing her opera career," and I say "My story about him touches on that—his commercials," and she says "You saw him in a waiter's uniform at a restaurant and asked him for a menu when he was actually performing in a commercial?" and I say "It was at the Belvedere Fountain Café in Central Park—eight years and a few months ago, and he was resting between shoots; I remember it distinctly. My oldest boy was still in that little carrying sack over my chest—a Snugli—and probably snoozing," and she says "Oh, that's lovely, precious, and I can just see it, and we never even talked about your own family—are there any others?" and I say "My wife, a younger boy," and she says "Two—you got your hands full," and I say "Not so far, and yours turned out okay, or will—but Leonard . . . he told you he saw me with my baby?" and she says "Someone else I know had the same experience with him in a Soho restaurant—it's hilarious how he's typecast," and she laughs. "But he's such a sweetie—they should have had children when they could." "And Myron Rock?" and she says "Three kids, two divorces, slew of groupies." "I meant—but anyway, so you see him," and she says "When I come in sometimes—he in fact said he got a nice letter from you regarding his last book," and I say "I saw it advertised and wrote him care of his publisher something like 'Glad you hung in there, I couldn't.'" "So you haven't?" and I say "Gave it up for good some fifteen years ago, though I'm always reading it." "Any success?" and I say "A few times at reading it." "Ho-ho, but the one you wrote him about was his best, didn't you think?" and I say "Flat, forced, fake and familiar and with a stupid commercial title—*In Bed With Clark Gable* or something." "It was *Hollywood Here I Come*—his experiences screenwriting there, and a double meaning which you, the teacher, got, if not even a triple, but why'd you write him if you thought it so bad?" and I say "Just what I told you: because he stuck with it—crummy book but a book every three years or so and apparently able to live fairly well off his work, which I would have loved but didn't have whatever it is to do it." "So you never had a book published?" "One little measly one—I've plenty of copies I bought for a dollar each so I'll send you one if you like." "That'd be nice, thanks, and your friend Henry?" "Henry Greenfield?" "Yes." "How's he doing?" "That's right," and I say "I see him about once every eighteen months— he's completely changed: skinny instead of stocky, shaved his skull, big beard, wears an earring and kiddy clothes and has become a visual artist—he made enough in antiques to retire—and he and Gilda split up after twenty-five years," and she says "I liked her, lots of spunk and smarts, even if she didn't care for me— remember?" and I say "Even where and when she said it—they and I were subbing together at a Bronx junior high school and it was on the train to work and she said 'What do you think Ramona has against me?'" "I never had anything against her." "I know, which I told her then—I think it was all out of envy—your profession, personableness, income and that you didn't have to hack it out as a sub every day. Anyway, I see her now even more than I do Henry—he's become a bit too odd, the new face and costume each time and hip talk and woman after woman after woman and each five years younger than the previous one till they're now younger than his daughter, who's first-year med school, by the way." "How could it be—shy little Phoebe?" "Little Phoebe who's about ten feet tall." "In size?" "Both . . . but how's your old acting-school friend Thalia?" and she says "Thelma—it was at her party, in fact, where we met, wasn't it?" and I say "It was a friend of my brother Peter's, which is how I came to it, and you came with Thelma, so maybe she knew the host or someone who knew him— that was some night, Christmas Eve, snowing, and you and I talked awhile and then left for midnight services at Saint Patrick's because you wouldn't mind praying and I'd always wanted to be on the line there outside with someone like you who'd cuddle into me because of the cold, and it happened—well, I've told you this before, nothing like fantasies realized," and she says "I think you told me it that very night," and I say "It was the same with my wife, almost same circumstances, but a New Year's Eve party I met her at." "Your brother invited you?" "No, he was dead by then—I was actually invited by the hosts and saw her, my future wife—" "What's her name?" "Carolyn." "And your boys'?" "Andrei and Daniel, two writers she's written about and admires and even knew, I think—and fell in love at first sight there—I did— In other words, at the party I was immensely attracted to her and introduced myself or had someone introduce us—" "Surely you remember," and I say "I introduced myself and asked whom she knew—something dumb like that—woman or boy friend giving the party and found out she came with a woman friend, as you had twenty years before, and was single." "What would you have done if she wasn't?" "Probably made a pass at her, which I think I was still doing then—I know I was: if I couldn't get the whole works then maybe just a quick fling. Though looking back at it it's not something I've liked in myself and don't especially care for when men do it to Carolyn at parties and gatherings of various sorts." "It's happened that often with her?" "Four or five times I know of—she's very pretty with an attractive figure besides whatever else she gives off." "What do you do when it happens?" and I say "Well, she tells me it after, but once I overheard it. 'You're married?' the guy said, 'well that's too bad'—something like that—a sort of wry disappointment, which I think is what I used to use, since it doesn't completely cut you off, but with her, you see—this confusion the men have I mean—it's also because she doesn't wear a wedding band." "Why not?" and I say "She lost it doing the laundry in our building's laundry room." "How long ago?" "Three years," and she says "She should get one because then maybe fewer men would make passes and you'd be less agitated by it," and I say "I'm not really agitated by it and I've made a couple of passes or approaches or whatever you call it to women with wedding bands—before I was married, of course—though truth is when I made them I didn't look at their wedding fingers for a band, and besides, some married women wear it on the right hand

Russian-style—I just looked at my own hands to see which one the band's normally on—and some unmarried women wear the band as a precaution of some sort, a safety device—I'm not getting the right word, but some strategy." "Certainly not a strategy to attract men." "Well, some men might be more attracted to married women, less of a threat." "The husband could be a threat if he's there," and I say "True, true, anyway, she wasn't married, so didn't have a ring and doesn't now." "But you seem happily married." "Very much so," and she says "That's wonderful—Josh and I were too for a few years but then we should have split up ten years ago but didn't because of the children." "Must be difficult living with someone you don't want to live with," and she says "Oh, despite what I might have said we remained compatible, we're still compatible, he's a dear, fair very decent sweet guy—no arguments or complaints, never yells—just he was always uninteresting and invariable, if I can speak openly. If you don't like this, please say so," and I say "No, it's all right, what?" and she says "No spark is what I mean and little to no curiosity outside of his own work and the one thing we were interested and involved in together, the well-being of our kids—maybe the first couple of years before we married he was interesting or living with him was or seemed to be, but after that, well . . . I just couldn't see myself going through ten to twenty more years of a totally dull compatible marriage with a boring lifeless man and most of those years without the distractions of kids—I in fact thought it'd make me nuts—I know, I know, I've made my point all too clear and probably contradicted myself several times and sound to you repellently faddish, so excuse me." "It's not that," and she says "Not what?" "Everything you said, and I'm sorry for what you both have gone through," and she says "Don't worry about that, Josh finally realized with me our marriage was a tremendous mistake and is much happier with the situation now, but can you—I mean, you can be sure, to get back to what we were originally saying—in fact I still wear it, left hand, but not anymore the engagement ring, to feel safer on the street as you said—but that gives away what I was about to say, which is that I always wore my wedding band, no matter what I thought of my marriage, and I also once lost it but bought a new one in days," and I say "So you think it odd my wife doesn't replace hers?" "Not odd or no odder than that you don't encourage her to or get her a new one—after all, yours sounds like a wonderful marriage," and I say "It is, with minor problems of course." "Like what?" "Like what everybody must go through when they don't go through real marital problems—minor, too normal to describe—but if I just went out and got her a wedding band it would have to match mine like the original." "Not really; mine didn't—though if you insisted, then just as easy: you show yours and they match it." "I don't have her size." "Ask her—eliminates the surprise, but you forfeit that," and I say "Who knows his or her finger size? For it wasn't that simple when we got our fingers measured by the man we ordered them from." "Then you go back to him and he probably has a record of her size, so you can still pull off the surprise." "Fingers don't expand?" "If you get a lot heavier perhaps, but the way you spoke about her, she hasn't." "She's actually lost weight, and she was never heavy, since we married." "Then if she hasn't lost a lot there should be no problem, or who knows, because maybe she likes not wearing one." "What do you mean?" and she says "Some people don't like wearing anything on their fingers or around their necks and wrists and so on." "That's what you meant? It didn't seem so," and she says "Then maybe I don't know what I meant—really, what's the difference? Because there was nothing to it," and I say "Of course, that's not what I was saying—by the way, how'd you get my number?" and she says "Well, it's a story— I called your school—" "How'd you know I worked there?" "I bumped into Ronnie Salter a few years ago—that's what I should have started with—" "Ronnie, how's he doing?" and she says "Oh, gosh, I forget—driving a cab, maybe not that—a fire fighter, did he say? I really forget, but I asked him, or he just came out and told me where you taught, but the school always rang your office and nobody was in, till I finally got wise and asked for your department and called it and they said you had exactly two office hours a week and they couldn't give out your home phone number, but it was listed in Manhattan Information under your wife's maiden name, and they gave me it. I thought it'd be nice renewing contact with you—I hate losing touch with people I truly considered close friends—how many are there of those? And we go back nearly thirty years." "More I bet, and that's very nice of you." "And so I thought we could get together again. I'd love hearing about you, your wife and what she does, and children and things," and I say

"No, it's good and I want you to meet her and if we could get the timing right, the kids." "I'd love it." "You still get to New York regularly then?" and she says "From time to time, mostly on business." "And what's that?—but this must be costing you," and she says "Don't worry about it—think of all I've saved these years without calling you. I own a pottery shop where we sell and teach—I've a couple of women in with me," and I say "You were interested in pottery, that's right, almost as much as acting." "Not only interested. For many years after I gave up acting it was all I did—study, dug my own mud. I even showed, not that anything came of it—so we both, you could say, went through the same thing, but I stuck with it though mostly now running the shop and teaching it, not something I especially enjoy anymore but I can't for the rest of my life rely on Josh even if he wanted me to," and I say "I can understand, you want to be independent." "I have to be." "Right, you have no choice—so, would you like to have lunch here?" and she says "Sure, it's why I called, to see you and talk." "What I mean is you'd have to come here, if you're going to meet Carolyn and the kids, since we have no car and I never get up there." "I know—I can't plan anything for a couple of weeks but some time after that—let me give you my number and I've got yours and your office hours and one of us will phone the other," and I take down her number and in case I lose it, I say, her address and she says "Well, I've really loved this, and when you see your mother please don't forget that special hug from me," and I say "I'm sure she'll remember you, thanks, and I'll be talking to you," and she says "Same here, good-by," and we hang up.

I go into the living room and say "Excuse me, can I butt in on your work a minute?" and she says "What, your call?" and I say "You wouldn't believe who it was," and she says "Ramona Bauer, woman you almost married, one of your three or four great loves and first one of your adult life—I heard you shout her name out," and I say "It's been what?" and count back in my head. "Twenty-two years—I remember because to see her I borrowed a car from the other associate editor of the two dick magazines I worked for then, and I only worked there a few months before I got the radio news job. She was living with her boyfriend—now he's her husband, though they're divorcing," and she says "That's interesting, because you've said she called you a number of times like that when she was divorcing or breaking up after a long relationship." "I didn't know I told you that," and she says "Everything, you've told me everything, or at least you said you have, about all your old flames." "What else I tell you about her?" and she says "What else is there? Everything is everything. First one to get on top of you, second or third female to break your heart. That she was reading *Dear Theo* when you met her. She taught you how to smoke a pipe and then told you your breath stunk from it, so you stopped and never smoked anything again. Her artist father, actor brother, playwright mother." "That's right, they were—the parents. Very glamorous sophisticated people," and she says "You told me that too. How they opened you to things you'd never experienced before—way of life, way to live, martinis, fireplaces, roasted whole duck. Did she ask about me?" "Come to think of it, nothing particular—mostly friends we both knew, and my mother and brothers and sisters. But she said I seemed very happily married and asked your name and I think what you did. And the kids." "Why do you think she called?" and I say "To renew our friendship, she said, because you know, besides being lovers we were good friends." "Also, to see if you were still married, I'd say, or had ever got married, really," and I say "No, she knew—she spoke to someone who told her of my teaching, so he must have mentioned my marriage." "How long ago?" and I say "A few years, I think." "Then maybe she thought you could be divorced, as I said, or in the process of getting one. Just, in other words, finding out where you were on those—if you were content in your marriage, even, for all we know." "What do you mean?" and she says "After everything you've said about her, she could be a little sly one, and she might have recently been thinking of you. Because you were always in good shape, thought you might still be in good shape. Remembered your ardor, shall we say?, your intellect, that you were good-looking and always loved kids and now have a secure job—tenure, she might have heard—and she has them, right, kids?" and I say "Two, teens," and she says "Well then, that's important, your loving kids, but could be I'm stretching things too far. But are you very happily married, as she said?" and I say "Don't be silly, you know I am. Very. Mostly. Sure. What are you going on for?" "I don't know. Sly old lover calls out of the blue after twenty-two years?" "No, she's more sincere than that." "Then sincere old lover calls, but probably a little bit wily too. I bet she doesn't call you again—you make plans to meet?" "No, but she said something about getting together in a couple of weeks. She's busy, something. She'd come down from New Haven—I told her I couldn't go up." "How'd you do that?" and I say "Young kids in school, I like to pick them up, and you're very involved on your project, and I've lots of work to do too. And she wouldn't come down just to see me but because she comes down periodically, on business—she owns, with some women, a pottery studio or shop. Teaches it, sells, probably exhibits—it's what she was also interested in, besides acting." "Well, I bet she never calls and I bet if you called her in two weeks she'd say she's tied up and she'll get back to you and never would and would hope you got the message. You're not free; you're not a possibility." "One good thing to say about that is she's not trying to steal me away from you." "If she thought things weren't going well with us, who knows? But let her. I wouldn't do anything to stop it." "You wouldn't at least cry, for that sure as hell would get me running back? Or say to me if I walk out once I'm gone for good as far as you're concerned?" "But that wouldn't be the case. I'd put up with your leaving once, doing it to someone behind my back, having a sneaky sloppy affair while still living here. Twice, I don't think so. But once, I'd probably let you back if someone didn't come into my life in the meantime, not that there'd be much chance with two kids growing up and so many totally free much younger women around." "A lot of men would like a mature beautiful woman with kids," and she says "Beautiful mature twenty-three and beautiful mature forty-three are very different things. So, given the choice, who would—you?" "I did, though admittedly they were twenty-eight, thirty, thirty-three or so, but no older. And, true too, they each only had one kid. But two I don't think would stop most men—I doubt it would have stopped me—and you look young and your body and mind are youthful." "Even with the ones you lived with, young as they were, you didn't stay with them long, and the one you did, you didn't marry. You in fact told me a short time after we met that one of my attractions was that I was single and childless and of childbearing age." "It had nothing to do with the children, I don't think, why these women and I broke up. I wanted to change the pattern with you, as if my luck would change if I did. It was actually hard leaving these women, because of their kids. I ended up loving the children much more than I ever did them. Anyway, she's not out after me—or wasn't, before she called. She's smart and knows that some of whatever it was that kept us from sticking together the first two rounds probably still exists. Our backgrounds, what we both think serious and so on. Too many differences, intellectual and otherwise. Acting. I mean, how could I have thought I could live the rest of my life with an actress, and she with a hermit who likes to work in a hole? She needed someone to really laugh and joke and go to a lot of movies and plays and socialize with, nothing I liked doing and apparently her last husband didn't either, and she still seems that way. She'd be bored with me and I probably would in ways with her. The initial fleshy and bubbly attraction might still be there but that might be all. Maybe I'm wrong. Besides that, if I took up with someone now, though of course it's never going to happen, I'd want to have a child by her, since I'm sure you'd take ours. I know, I know. I could see them almost every weekend and month in the summer and so on—holidays for a couple days and probably when it was more convenient to you than me—but it wouldn't be enough. I'd want one around all the time." "So, we're not going to split up— okay. And you had a good conversation with her?" and I say "Very much. You know me, I'm terrible on the phone, almost afraid of it, and this one was easy and what I like best from it—plenty of info, several short bios, some laughs, lots of filling in. Except maybe it was an oversight on her part or some minor quirk not to ask more about you. I admit that. But now and then we all forget what we're supposed to do in certain situations, even things we want to and have prepared ourselves for. The mind slips. I wouldn't make anything more of it."

The next day I see my mother and say "Remember Ramona Bauer?" and she says "Who's that?" "Woman I was engaged to when I was in my early twenties and whom I saw and was head over heels for for years—blonde, an actress. Very pretty. Had a couple of good Broadway parts, and one of them when I was seeing her— I even took you to the play. Neither of us liked it but we thought she was very good. Then she broke off the engagement a month or so before we were to be married. This happened during my second time around with her, but I don't want to make this any more confusing than it has to be." "No, the engagement breakoff I don't remember, though it seems something I would. And usually I'm good at things from that far back." "It was going to be at her parents' house in Connecticut. A small wedding, which was what we wanted; maybe thirty, forty people." "I'm sorry, it still doesn't register. Maybe I'm not functioning well today." "Ramona Bauer, Mom. How many Ramonas have I known?" "None, it seems, as far as I'm concerned. Maybe try being more specific about her looks other than for her being pretty and blonde. Anything particularly striking or noticeable about her size or face or manners then?" "Long hair. And a real light blond, not dirty or honey-colored or anything like that. Usually combed straight back and hanging over her shoulders or tied on top into that bun that dancers wear; I think it's called or was called then a chignon. About your height, maybe a couple of inches taller." "So my height when I was her age." "That's right. And vivacious, very lively, energetic and a very distinctive voice, though I don't know if I can describe it. A bit throaty, though not from smoking, and every word clear. A trained actress, so she enunciates, but not affected." She shakes her head. "This might help. Dad objected to her because of her religion, but you didn't. You both even met her folks, took them to dinner after we got engaged. At a restaurant in the Empire State Building on the ground floor. The Showboat, I think it was called. They might even have had some Dixieland music—I say that because of the restaurant's name, and somehow the image of these guys playing comes up. Her father was an artist, didn't do well, but came from old money, which there wasn't much of by the time it came to his turn. Her mother was a playwright with a couple of hits in the forties and fifties. Or maybe just the forties, and I think both of those were musicals she only did the lyrics or book for. 'Nelson' his name was, very handsome eloquent man. I forget her name but I think she also wrote children's books or was trying to get one published when I met Ramona, plus still doing her plays. You in fact—I just remembered this—at this restaurant, said to her father that you immediately can see whom Ramona takes after. He wasn't blond—neither was her mother—but their small noses and green eyes and almost everything else about their faces was the same." "None of it," she says. "You'd think one small part of it would come back. It has to be the day. I had a bad night." "I'm sorry. Anyway, she called me, Ramona did." "What for?" "Because she still considers me her friend after twenty years and would like to see me." "She married?" and I say "Getting divorced." "She wants to hook up with you again." "No, she doesn't. That's all over." "Sure she does. You have a good job, for life if you want. She probably has lots of expenses and mouths to feed and she's lonely again." "No, she knows I'm happily married. And her husband—one she's divorcing—is a successful movie or TV producer or something with public TV. He does well, anyway, from what I could make out, and I'm sure will support her and the two children very well. If she needs it, I'm saying, since she has her own independent work." "You're still good-looking—" "How would she know that, not that I am." "You are. Don't underestimate yourself. And why you so sure she knew you were married? She wanted to get her hooks into you and, knowing you're married now, she still might. People get desperate when they reach a certain age." "She's not like that. Everything she said on the phone and that I know about her says that." "How old is she?" "Fifty-three, since she was seven months younger than I. Born in January." "So she knows that nobody's going to be interested in her now or at least not like someone who was in love with her and she ran away from." "She broke off the engagement, she didn't run away. In fact I saw her for a little while after that and then every now and then for about a year. She decided—what did she decide? Well, it was like Dad said. That our two religions would make us incompatible after a while, since at the time she was so seriously involved with hers. Also, that she knew I'd want children right away—I did, mostly to hold her down; I knew she didn't want to get married then—and she wanted to wait till she was in her thirties, so she could continue with her acting work. And that's just what she did, though she got married a couple of times before this long one. No, I'm sure she wants to see me just to resume our friendship. We were very good that way and did sporadically see each other as friends for almost ten years after we stopped being lovers the last time. And nostalgia—people do funny things because of it." "Like what?" and I say "I don't know—call up a friend thirty years later on his birthday from ten thousand miles away because it just flashed to them. She didn't; she's in Connecticut. Anyway, she said she has the fondest memories of you especially. That you were always wonderful to her—generous, warm, uncritical—and that she wants me to give you a big hug and kiss from her." "I don't want a hug from her. I don't know her, I don't remember her, and I don't trust her. Now, if Carolyn wants you to give me a hug and kiss from her, that I'll accept."

FLYING

She was fooling around with the plane's door handle. I said "Don't touch that, sweetheart, you never know what can happen." Suddenly the door disappeared and she flew out and I yelled "Judith" and saw her looking terrified at me as she was being carried away. I jumped out after her, smiled and held out my arms like wings and yelled "Fly like a bird, my darling, try flying like a bird." She put out her arms, started flying like me and smiled. I flew nearer to her and when she was close enough I pulled her to my body and said "It's not so bad flying like this, is it? It's fun. You hold out one arm and I'll hold out one of mine and we'll see where we can get to." She said "Daddy, you shouldn't have gone after me, you know that," and I said "I wouldn't let you out here all alone. Don't worry, we'll be okay if we keep flying like this and, once we're over land, get ourselves closer and closer to the ground."

The plane by now couldn't be seen. Others could, going different ways, but none seemed to alter their routes for us no matter how much waving I did. It was a clear day, blue sky, no clouds, the sun moving very fast. She said "What's that?" pointing down and I said "Keep your arm up, we have to continue flying." She said "I am, but what's that?" and I said "Looks like a ship but it's probably an illusion." "What's an illusion?" and I said "What a time for word lessons; save them for when we get home. For now just enjoy the flying and hope for no sudden air currents' shifts." My other arm held her tightly and I pressed my face into hers. We flew like that, cheek to cheek, our arms out but not moving. I was worried because I hadn't yet come up with any idea to help us make a safe landing. How do we descend, how do we land smoothly or crash-land without breaking our legs? I'll hold her legs up and just break mine if it has to come to that. She said "I love you, Daddy, I both like you and love you and always will. I'm never going to get married and move away from home." I said "Oh well, one day you might, not that I'll ever really want you to. And me too to you, sweetie, with all that love. I'm glad we're together like this. A little secret though. For the quickest moment in the plane I thought I wouldn't jump out after you, that something would hold me back. Now nothing could make me happier than what I did."

We left the ocean and we were over cliffs and then the wind shifted and we were being carried north along the coast. We'd been up at almost the same distance from water and land for a long time and I still had no idea how to get down. Then along the coastal road I saw my wife driving our car. Daniel was in the front seat, his hand sticking out the window to feel the breeze. The plane must have reported in about the two people sucked out of the plane, and when Sylvia heard about it she immediately got in the car and started looking for us, thinking I'd be able to take care of things in the air and that the wind would carry us east.

"Look at them, sweetheart, Mommy and Daniel. He should stick his arm in; what he's doing is dangerous." She said "There aren't any other cars around, so it can't hurt him." "But it should be a rule he always observes, just in case he forgets and sticks it out on a crowded highway. And a car could suddenly come the other way. People drive like maniacs on these deserted roads and if one got too close to him his arm could be torn off." "But the car would be going the other way—wouldn't it?—so on Mommy's side, not his," and I said "Well, the driver of another car going their way could suddenly lose his head and try and pass on the right and get too close to Daniel's arm. —Daniel," I screamed, "put your arm back right now. This is Daddy talking." His arm went back in. Sylvia stopped the car, got out and looked up and yelled "So there you are. Come back now, my darlings; you'll get yourselves killed." "Look at her worrying about us, Judith—that's nice, right? — Don't worry, Sylvia," I screamed, "we're doing just fine, flying. There's no feeling like it in the world, we're both quite safe, and once I figure out a way to get us down, we will. If we have to crash-land doing it, don't worry about Judith—I'll hold her up and take the whole brunt of it myself. But I think it's going to be some distance from here, inland or on the coast, so you just go home now and maybe we'll see you in time for dinner. But you'll never be able to keep up with us the way this wind's blowing, and I don't know how to make us go slower." "You sure you'll be all right?" she yelled, and I said "I can hardly hear you anymore, but yes, I think I got everything under control."

We flew on, I held her in my arm, kissed her head repeatedly, thinking if anything would stop her from worrying, that would. "You sure there's nothing to worry about, Daddy? I mean about what you said to Mommy," and I said "What are you doing, reading my mind? Yes, everything's okay, I'm positive." We continued flying, each with an arm out, and by the time night came we were still no closer to or farther away from the ground.

MAN, WOMAN, AND BOY

They're sitting. "It's wrong," she says. He says "I know." She stands, he does right after her. "It's all wrong," she says. "I know," he says, "but what are we going to do about it?" She goes into the kitchen, he follows her. "It almost couldn't be worse," she says. "Between us—how could it be? I don't see how." "I agree," he says, "and I'd like to change it from bad to better but I don't know what to do." She pours them coffee. She puts on water for coffee. She fills the kettle with water. She gets the kettle off the stove, shakes it, looks inside and sees there's only a little water in it, turns on the faucet and fills the kettle halfway and then. And then? "Do you want milk, sugar?" she says. This after the water's dripped through the grounds in the coffee maker, long after she said "I'm making myself coffee, you want some too?" He nodded. Now he says "You don't know how I like it by now?" "Black," she says. "Black as soot, black as ice. Black as the ace of spades, as the sky, a pearl, black as diamonds." "Whatever," he says, "whatever are you talking about?" "Just repeating something you once said. How you like your coffee." "I said that? Those, I mean—I said any of them? Never. You know me. I don't say stupid or foolish things, I try not to talk in clichés, I particularly dislike similes in my speech, and if I'm going to make a joke, I know beforehand it's going to get a laugh. But to get back to the problem." "The problem is this," she says. "We're two people, in one house, with only one child, and I'm not pregnant with a second. We have a master bedroom and one other bedroom, so one for us and one for the child. We have no room for guests. We have no guest room. The sofa's not comfortable enough to sleep on and doesn't pull out into a bed. We have no sleeping bag for one of us to sleep on the floor. I don't want our boy to sleep in the master bed with one of us while the other sleeps in his bed. One of us has to go, is what I'm saying." "I understand you," he says. "The problem's probably what you said. It is, let's face it. One of us has to go because both of us can't stay, and traditionally it's been the man. But I don't want to go, I'd hate it. Not so much to leave you but him. Not at all to leave you. I'm being honest. Don't strike out against me for it, since it's not something I'm saying just to hurt you." "I wouldn't," she says. "I like honesty. And the feeling's mutual, which I'm also not saying just to get back at you for what you said. But I'm not leaving the boy and traditionally the man is, in situations like this, supposed to, or simply has. We've seen it. Our friends, and friends of friends we've heard of, who have split up. The child traditionally stays with the woman. And it's easier, isn't it, for the one without the child to leave than the one who stays with it, and also ends up being a lot easier on the child. So I hope that's the way it'll turn out. I think we both agree on that or have at least agreed on it in our conversation just now." "Our conversation, which is continuing," he says. "Our conversation, which should conclude. It wouldn't take you too long to pack, would it?" "You know me," he says, "I never acquired much. Couple of dress shirts, two T-shirts, three pairs of socks, not counting the pair I'm wearing, three or four handkerchiefs, a tie. Two undershorts, including the one on me, pair of work pants in addition to the good pants I've on. Sports jacket to match the good pants, work jacket and coat, hat, muffler, boots, sneakers, the shoes I'm wearing, and that should be it. Belt, of course. Bathing suit and running shorts. Anything I leave behind—some books except the one I'm reading and will take—I can pick up some other time.

The tie, in fact, I can probably leave here; I never use it." "You might," she says. "Anyway, it's small enough to take and not use. Take everything so you'll be done with it. So you're off then? Need any help packing?" "For that amount of stuff? Nah. But one last time?" "What, one last time?" she says. "A kiss, a smooch, a feel, a hug, a little bit of pressing the old family flesh together, okay?" "You want to make me laugh? I'll laugh. Cry? I'll do that too. Which do you want me to do?" "Okey-doke, I got the message and was only kidding." "Oh yes, for sure, only kidding, you." "What's that supposed to mean?" he says. "Oh you don't know, for sure, oh yes, you bet." "If you're referring to that smooch talk, what I meant was I'd like to be with my child for a few minutes before I go. To hug, squeeze, kiss and explain that I'm not leaving him but you. That I'll see him periodically, or really as much as I can— every other day if you'll let me. You will let me, right?" "For the sake of him, of course, periodically. More coffee?" "No thanks," he says. "Then may I go to my room while you have this final get-together with him? Not final; while you say good-by for now?" "Go on. I won't steal him."

They move backward, she to the couch, he to the chair. They never drank coffee, never made it; never had that conversation. They're both reading, or she is and he has the book on his lap. Their son's on the floor putting a picture puzzle together. It's a nice domestic scene, he thinks, quiet, the kind he likes best of all. Fire going in the fireplace—he made it. A good one too, though fires she makes are just as good. It doesn't give off much heat, fault of the fireplace's construction, but looks as if it does and is beautiful. Thermostat up to sixty-eight so, with the fire, high enough to keep the house warm, cozy. He has tea beside him on the side table. On the side table beside him. Beside his chair. A Japanese green tea, and he's shaved fresh ginger into it. Tea's now lukewarm. Tastes it; it is. He's been thinking these past few minutes and forgot about the tea. She has a cup of hot water with lemon in it. Not hot now—she might even have finished it—but was when he gave it to her. About ten minutes ago she said "Strange as this must sound"—he'd said he was making himself tea, would she like some or anything with boiling water?—"it's all I want. I wonder if it means I'm coming down with something." He said "You feel warm?" "No." "Anything ache—limbs, throat, extremities?" "Nope. I guess I'm not," and resumed reading. "What could you be coming down with, Mommy?" the boy said. "Your mommy means with a cold," he said. "Oh," the boy said and went back to his puzzle. I wonder, the man thinks, what that long parting scene I imagined means. It's not like that with us at all. We're a happy couple, a relatively happy one. Hell, happier than most it seems, more compatible and content and untroubled than most too. I still love her. Do I? Be honest. I still do. Very much so. Very much? Oh, well, most days not as passionately or crazily as I loved her when I first met her or the first six months or so of our being together before we got married or even the first six months or so of our marriage, but close enough to that. She still excites me. Very much so. Physically, intellectually. We make love a lot. About as much as when we first met, or after the first month we met. She often initiates it. Not because I don't. Lots of times she does when I'm thinking of initiating it but she starts it first. She doesn't seem dissatisfied. I'm not too. What's there to be dissatisfied about? A dozen or so years since we met and we still go at it like kids, or almost like kids—like adults, anyone—what I'm saying is, almost as if sometimes it's the first. I have fantasies about other women but what do they mean? Meaning, they don't mean much: I had them a week after I met her, they're fleeting and they probably exist just to make it even better with her, but probably not. They exist. That's the way I am. As long as I don't act on them, which I'd never do, for why would I? Which is what I'm saying. And she tells me she loves me almost every day. Tells me almost every day. And almost every night one of the last things she says to me, in the dark or just before or after she turns off the light, is "I love you, dearest." And I usually say "I love you too," which is true, very much so: I do, and then we'd briefly kiss and maybe later, maybe not, after I put down my reading, make love. So why'd I think of that scene? Just trying it out? Wondering how I'd feel? How would I? Awful, obviously. I couldn't live without her. Or I could but it'd be difficult, very, extremely trying, probably impossible, or close. And without the boy? Never. As I said in the scene, I want to see him every day. He's such a good kid. I want to make him breakfast every morning till he's old enough to make his own, help him with his homework when he wants me to and go places with him—museums, the park, play ball with him, take walks with him—with him and her. Summer vacations, two to three weeks here or there, diving off rafts, long swims with him alongside me. Things like that. Libraries. He loves libraries and children's bookstores. Really odd that I thought of that scene then. Just trying it out as I said, that's all, or I suppose.

He gets up and gets on the floor and says "Need any help?" "No, Dad, thanks. If I do I'll tell you." "Sure now?" "Positive. I like to figure things out myself. That's the object of the puzzle, isn't it?" "Well, sometimes it's nice to do it with other people—it can be fun. But do what you want. And you're pretty good at this." "So far I am. I want to get up to one with a thousand pieces. This is only five hundred. But that's still two hundred more than the last one I did, which was two hundred fifty." "Two hundred fifty more than the last one," he says. "Two hundred fifty times two hundred fifty— no, I mean times two; or two hundred fifty plus another two hundred fifty equals—" "Five hundred. I know. Two hundred fifty times two hundred fifty is probably fifty thousand, or a hundred." "That's good. You're so smart." He touches the boy's cheek. "Okay, but if you need any help, whistle." "What for?" "I mean—it's just an expression, like what you said before: if you want me to help you'll tell me."

He goes over to his wife. She's reading and correcting manuscripts from her class. He puts his hand on top of her head. First he stood there thinking "Should I stay here till she notices me and looks up or should I put my hand on her head? On her head. Just standing here might seem peculiar to her. I'm sure if I was able to stand back and see myself standing here like this, it would seem peculiar." Now with his hand on her head he thinks "Actually, standing here with my hand on top of her head must also seem peculiar to her." Just as he's about to take his hand off, she looks up and grabs his hand with the one holding the pen. "Hello," she says. "Hello." "What's up?" she says. "Just admiring you." "You're a dear," she says. "You're the dear, a big one. I love you." "And I love you, my dearest." "And I love you very much," he says. "Very very." "Same with me, my dearest," she says. "Is that all? I mean, it's a lot and I like your hand here and holding it," and she squeezes it, "but may I return to my schoolwork unless you have anything further to say?" "Return, return," he says, and she pulls her hand away and holds the other side of the manuscripts with it.

"Oh, Daddy and Mommy said they love each other," the boy says. "That's right, we did," he says. "We said it and we do." "Are you just saying that to me?" the boy says. "Ask your mother." "Well, Mom?" "Well, what?" she says, looking up from her manuscripts. "Do you really love Daddy or are you—" "Yes, of course, such a question, what do you think? Now may I return to my work? Eight more essays to grade in a little bit under an hour. That's when I think I'll be too sleepy for anything but sleep." "Oh yes?" he says. "Leave your mother then to her readings." "Not before you both kiss on the lips." "You ask for so much," he says. "All right with you, ma'am?" he says to her. "Come ahither and adither," she says and moves her head up, he bends over and puts his lips on hers. He sticks the tip of his tongue in in a way that he's sure the boy won't be able to see. Their tongues touch, eyes close. His does he knows—the eyes. He opens his and sees hers are closed. Closes his and opens them quickly: still closed. "Okay, you proved it," the boy says. "You can stop now."

They move into the dining room. About an hour earlier, two. The three of them. They're seated, eating. He avoids looking at her, she him. He doesn't want to talk. When he wants something near her he nudges his son and points to it and his son gives it to him or he just reaches over, sometimes even has to stand up, and gets it himself. When she wants something near him she asks their son, though he always puts the thing he took back in the spot it was on. He's angry at her and doesn't want to just talk to his son and ignore her. Something she said. That he doesn't do enough of the housework. "Hell I don't," he said. "I do at least half or most of the work most of the time." That wasn't it. He and she didn't say that. What then? Said to her "You know, I hate saying this, but the house could be neater. You going to take umbrage, take." Said this to her about an hour before dinner. Soon after he came home from work. She'd got home from work a couple of hours earlier. The boy was in his room doing homework. Or that's what she said he was supposed to be there for. "You know I like order. That the chaos you prefer, or simply don't mind living with, gets to me viscerally sometimes. Forget the 'viscerally.' I can't stand chaos, it makes me nervous, temperamental, like cigarette smoke does. Forget the cigarette smoke. I just can't stand it." "Then tidy up the place," she said. "It's not just tidying up that's needed; it's also the dirt and dust." "Then clean up the place too." "I don't clean up enough? I do most of the cleaning, it seems, plus most of the clothes washing and shopping and making the beds and fixing up the boy's room and cleaning the bird's cage and feeding it every night and our cooking and dishwashing and all that crap, and I just think it's your turn. The food I see you've done, though I made the salad before I left. But the rest." "Okay, I'll clean up," she said. "I've been busy, I am busy, I did the dinner except the salad, set the table, it's been a rough day at school, I've helped our son with his long division for an hour and still have a mess of essays to grade, but if you think the distribution of housework's been un-equal, I'll do what you say. I wanted to say 'what the boss said,' but you might take umbrage. Umbrage; what a word." She cleaned up the living room and dining room. When she started to he said "I didn't mean now." Tidied up, swept the floors and rugs, dusted and polished the furniture, straightened the many books on the shelves, rubbed some stains on the wooden floor with a solution till she got them out. It looks and smells a lot better, he thought, place isn't a complete jumble, but she's making me feel guilty and she knows it. Why doesn't she do it periodically, as I do, and then it wouldn't come to this? "Do" meaning the cleaning; "this" being the disorder, dirty house, argument. The food was cooking, din-ner was. He didn't want to eat with the two of them feeling about each other like this, but what could he say: "I don't want to eat right now, you go ahead without me," after she'd cooked it and just cleaned part of the house, and he'd, so to speak, started the argument? He'd come home mad because of something that hap-pened at the office—more pettiness there, nothing that should have upset him. He took it out on her—might have taken it out on the boy if he'd been around—which isn't to say the place wasn't a visual assault when he got there, but it certainly wasn't enough of one to start an argument over, especially when he knew she'd taught most of the day and he could see she'd done some work at home: dinner, scrap paper scattered about showing she'd helped the boy with his long division. Besides, it just wasn't something that warranted arguing over anytime. He'd gone to work mad be-cause this morning in bed—it all could have stemmed from this—he'd wanted to make love. One of those mornings: dreamt of love-making, woke up thinking of lovemaking, wanted very much to do it. She mumbled "Too tired, sweetie," and moved her neck away from his lips. He persisted. "I said I'm tired, too much so, don't want to, please let me sleep, I need it." Usually she gave in, even when she didn't feel like it. She knew it'd only take him a few minutes when he was like this and she could take the easiest and least involved position and wouldn't even have to move to it since she was in it now—on her side with her back to him—and that he'd want to get out of bed right after to wash up, exercise, have coffee and read the paper, and prepare the breakfast table for their son and her. He pressed into her, put a hand on her breast through the nightgown, other hand between her legs. She had panties on. He hadn't known. He started to pull them down. "What, huh?" she said, as if startled awake. "Don't, dammit. I said I didn't want to and I certainly feel less like it now. Do it to yourself if you're so horny, but with me it'd be like with a corpse." "A corpse isn't warm." "Please?" "And I'm not horny; I just want you." "Sure," she said. "Oh yeah, you bet, oh boy," and moved a few inches away from him. "Bloody Christ," he said and got out of bed. "Bitch," he said softly but he thought loud enough for her to hear. She didn't respond, eyes were closed, she looked asleep. Faking it maybe, but who cares? They didn't talk at breakfast, which he ate standing up at the stove, she at the table he'd set. And he didn't look at her when he left for work. Put on his coat, got his briefcase, kissed his son, left. The previous day during dinner they'd had an argument. Her mother had said to him on the phone "Are you treating my daughter nicely? Remember, she's our only child, one in a zillion, and I always want her treated well because nobody in the world deserves it better." "Have you asked either of us if she's been treating me nicely?" he said. "What a question," she said. Then "Let me talk to her if she's there—it's why I called." His wife later asked him what he'd said that made her mother so mad, and it started. "She's too nosy sometimes and she expects sensible gentle answers to these impossible, often hostile questions, and then she dismisses me as if I'm her houseboy-idiot." "You don't know how to talk to her and you never liked her and you don't know how to act civilly to anyone you don't like." "Is that right," he said, and so on. That morning he'd wanted to make love and they did. After, she said "Nothing really gets started with me when we make it lately, and I end up so frustrated. You—do you mind my saying this?—

for the most part do it too quickly. You have to warm me up more and concentrate on the right spots, especially if you suddenly come on me unprepared, like when I'm asleep." "Listen, we're all responsible for our own orgasms," he said. "The hell we are." "I didn't mean it the way it might have come out, but we are to a certain degree, don't you think?" "You meant it and you show it," she said. "Just get yours, buster, and let whoever it is burn." "What 'whoever it is'?" he said. "It's only you." "Don't bullshit you don't know what I mean," she said, and so on. The previous day they fought about something, he forgets what: that she's been letting the gas gauge go almost to empty, that she took his stapler the other day and now he can't find it, that her personal trash in the bathroom wastebasket is starting to stink and it's her responsibility to dump it in the can outside or at least tie it up and stick it in the kitchen garbage bag. "So I forgot." "So from now on remember." "Don't fight," their son said, "please don't shout, please don't yell." They stopped but didn't talk to each other for a few hours. The previous night, when he was reading and at the same time falling asleep, she got into bed naked and said "You don't have to if you don't want to—no obligation," and he said "No no, I can probably do it," and they made love and went to sleep holding each other, she kissing his hand, he the back of her head. Further back. The boy's born, and he drops to his knees in the birthing room he's so excited. Further. They're getting married and they both break down during the ceremony and cry. Further. They meet. Sees her at a cocktail party, introduces himself: "You probably have better things to do than talk to me," and she says "What a line—no, why?" His first wife, girlfriends, first he was smitten with in grade school. He's a boy, and his parents are arguing bitterly at the dinner table. He puts his hands over his ears and yells "Stop, can't you ever stop screaming at yourselves?" "Don't do that," his father says, pulling his hands off his ears. "What are you, crazy?" And he says "Yes," or "You made me," or "Why shouldn't I be?" and runs out of the room. "Go after the maniac," and his brother goes after him and says "It's no good for me either when they're like that, so come on back." Hears further back. From his mother's stomach. "Filthy rotten bitch." "And you. Stupid, cheap, pigheaded, a pill. Get lost. I hate your guts." "Not as much as I hate yours. Here." "And what's that?" "What you wanted so much. Your allowance.

Take it and stick it up your ass," and so on. "Why'd I marry you?" and so on. "You don't think I ask that question too? With all I had and never any lip from anyone, what'd I need it for?" and so on.

He's in his chair, the man, wishing he'd made himself coffee or tea. Something hot to drink. He can think better with it. Son plays, wife reads. They'll probably make love tonight, he thinks. He's been nice all day, no arguments, she's smiled lovingly at him several times the last few hours. Kissed her when he got home, and she said "Ooh, that's some kiss; I love it." He can't wait. He's sure she'll come to bed ready. If she doesn't—well, how will he know? He can go to the bathroom and shake the case. Sometimes he can smell it on her too. The cream. Anyway, he can say—he's usually first in bed, usually reading—"I hope you're ready, I know I am." "Sure," she'll say if she isn't ready and go back to the bathroom. He loves her. They have their fights and disputes and sometimes he tells himself he hates her and doesn't want to live another second with her, but he really loves her. He should remember that. So beautiful. Still a very beautiful face. Her body still excites him. She's so smart, so good. He's lucky, particularly when he's so often a son of a bitch and fool. He should remember all that. He should call his mother now. Doesn't want to budge. Just wants to sit here remembering, digesting—something—the thoughts he just had about her. That he loves her. That no matter what, he loves her. "Time for bed," she says to their son. "Oh, I don't want to go yet," the boy says. "Do what your mother tells you," he says. "Okay," the boy says, "okay, but you don't have to talk rough." "I wasn't. And please clean up your puzzle. Nah, just forget it, it's late and you're going to bed; I'll do it." He looks at her. She's standing, her manuscripts are on the couch. Smiles at her. She smiles at him, he smiles back. The boy gets up and heads for the stairs. "Look," he says to her, "he's really going to bed without a fuss. What a kid." "I'll run his bath," she says, "you'll tell him a story after?" "I don't need anyone for that," the boy says. "I can fill my own tub—I know how much to—and I want to read by myself before I go to sleep." "You read?" the man says. "He reads?" to her. "Since when? I don't want him to. Soon I won't be able to do anything for him. He'll be brushing his own hair, combing his own teeth." "Daddy, you got those wrong. And I've been doing them a long time." "That's what I'm saying," he says. "Next you'll be cooking your own shoelaces, tying your own food. Go, go, don't let me stop you, big man," and blows a kiss at him. He didn't mean those first two to be switched around, but it turned out to be a good joke.

The boy runs upstairs. He gets on the floor, puts the—what do you call them? isolated, or incomplete, or unassembled or just-not-put-in-the-puzzle-yet—pieces in their box, doesn't know what to do with the partly completed puzzle, carefully slides it against the wall. Hears water running in the tub, lots of padding back and forth on the ceiling. "He's growing up so much," he says. "You haven't noticed before?" she says. "Of course, but the way he phrases things, and just now—no remonstrating." He sits beside her. "Mind?" "Go on." Puts his arm around her shoulder, pulls her to him. She looks at him. "Yes?" "This is the life," he says, "everything but the kid asleep." "Yes, it's very nice," and kisses his lips and goes back to reading. He continues looking at her. Wants to say "You're beautiful, you know; beautiful." Takes his arm away, for he feels it might be bothering her. She wants to concentrate. Good, she should. He leans his head back on the couch, looks at the ceiling. I go upstairs, he thinks. My son's in bed reading. He smells washed, his room's neat, he tidied it up without anyone asking. "All done for now?" I say. He puts the book on the floor and says "Forty-six; please remember the page for me?" "Will do. Goodnight, my sweet wonderful child," I say and kiss his lips, make sure the covers are over his shoulders. "Pillows all comfortable?" and he says "You could get them right, I don't mind." I fix the pillows, rest his head on them, turn the light off and go downstairs. "Like a beer or glass of wine?" I say. "If you'll share a bottle of beer with me," she says. We do. "I'm tired," I say. "Let's go to bed then," she says. We do. I'm in bed, naked, clothes piled beside me on the floor, glasses and book on my night table. She's still in— she's sitting on the other side of the bed, taking her clothes off. She was just in the bathroom a few minutes. "Dear," I say. "Not to worry," she says, "it's all taken care of. What's on your mind's on mine." All her clothes are off. I breathe deeply to see if I can smell her. I can: a little fresh cologne, cream she put in, something from her underarms. Or mine. I smell one when she's looking away. Nothing. "Can I shut off the light?" I say. "Please, I'm finished." I shut it off. She gets under the covers with me. We hug, kiss, rub each other very hard. She grabs me and I grab her. Something tells me it's going to be one of the best for me.

"Like a glass of wine, some beer?" he asks. "I don't want to get too sleepy," she says. "Maybe I can read a couple of more papers than I thought I could, so I won't have to do too many tomorrow." "Dad?" his son shouts from upstairs. "We're all out of toilet paper up here." "You checked the bathroom closet, the cabinet under the sink?" "Everyplace." "To the rescue." And he gets a roll out of the downstairs bathroom, runs upstairs, puts the roll in. He goes into his son's room. The boy's drawing at his desk, and he says "Don't you have to use the toilet?" "I did, but I was thinking of you and Mom." "That's very thoughtful, very. Come on now, though, you have to go to bed." The boy gets into bed. "Teeth all combed?" "Everything," the boy says. "You don't want the night light on?" "I don't need it anymore." "Good, that's fine, but if you change your mind, okay too. Good night, my sweet wonderful kid," and he bends down and kisses him on the lips, turns the light off.

He undresses, brushes his teeth, flosses, washes his face, washes his penis and behind with a washrag, washes the washrag with soap and hangs it on the shower rod, walks a few steps downstairs and says softly "Sweetheart, I'm going to bed now, to read—you coming up soon?" "No. And don't wait up for me. I'm thinking now I'll just do the whole bunch of them, no matter how long it takes. Good night." "Good night." He gets into bed, opens a book, reads, feels sleepy, puts the book down, looks at her side of the bed and thinks "Remember what you promised to think about before? What was it? Bet you forgot." Thinks. "Ah," he says when he re-members what it was. "It's true," he thinks, "I really love her." "You hear that, dear," he says low, "do you hear that? I can't wait till you get into bed so I can hold ya." He puts the book and glasses on the night table, shuts off the light, lies on his back to see if any-thing else comes into his head, shuts his eyes, turns over on his side, falls asleep.

CROWS

She went outside, came back in, pounded her head with her
knuckles several times, went outside again, looked and looked, nowhere to be seen, couldn't imagine what had happened, yelled
"Henry," and he appeared, his voice did, from the cellar. "Yes,
what's up? I'm down here." "Thank God," she said and held onto
the doors folded over and then the walls as she went down the
stone steps. "Don't leave me like that anymore, please." "Leave you
how?" he said. "Like that, like that," pointing upstairs. "Like what,
like what?" he said, painting a lawn chair, looking up at her for a
second. "Like leaving me. Tell me next time. You know how I am."
"No, I really don't, or not exactly. How are you? You're fine, I can
see. But you were worried. Don't be." "I was worried. When I call
for you, look for you, go up and downstairs and outside and down
the road and around the house for you? Well, I only called that
one time and I didn't go down the road looking for you, but I almost did." "Did you by chance ever think to call for me earlier or to
look down here? When you see the cellar doors open, assume I'm

down it." "You could have been elsewhere while airing the cellar out." "That's true," he said, painting, "you're right. I forgot that's what I do and it's just the kind of day for that."

She looked around. "I think we should build a staircase inside the house to the cellar. Then you could go up and down with ease, even evenings if you'd like, for there'd be a railing and light. And also not get wet in the rain if it's raining when you want to come here, or have to put boots on if it's snowing. And I wouldn't be searching franticly for you. I'd open the door to the cellar in the kitchen, let's say, and know by the sounds or the light on that you're down there." "Then we'd call the cellar a basement. I never want to have a basement in this house. Then we'd fix it up, put in a convertible couch and lamps and fixtures on the walls for more lamps and insulate it so guests would come, or for when they came, and a place to dump the grandkids when they were being too restless or loud. And fancy windows and then bars on the windows to protect our valuable lamps and grandkids from vandals and thieves. And the walls would have to be plastered smooth and then painted bright to cheer up the room, and the furnace would have to be concealed because it's an eyesore. And a drop ceiling to make believe we have no overhead pipes, and pictures in frames and so on. A mirror. A dehumidifier. A wine rack instead of the boxes the wine comes in I now use. Never. My parents had that, right down to the bar with two stools and a carbonated water tap, and it was disgusting. They had to clean it every other week. The floor—I forgot the floor—was linoleum, and when we left scuff marks on it we got reprimanded for it. I like the way it is. I open the cellar doors—clement or inclement weather, who cares? Climb down, do my work, single bulb dangling over the table, furnace like a furnace, no electrical outlets but the extension socket the light bulb's in, my sweater or vest or both if it's damp or cold, and once a year I use the old broom to brush away the spiders and spiderwebs and cobwebs." "But I get worried for you." "Then I'll tell you what, ask yourself why you do." "Because if I can't see or hear you I sometimes think something awful's happened to you." "Ask yourself this then: What could happen to me? I'm healthy. A heart attack? Hell, I could have got one when I was forty or fifty, and statistics say there was a better chance then, or is that just with a stroke? And I know my way around and don't risk injuries and accidents. If I got pains someplace that might seem unusual, and I know where those places are, I'd recognize the signs. So from now on, if you want me, look for me further. Upstairs, downstairs, outside, in. That's not much looking. Down the cellar—now that's looking, or down the road." "But you weren't down the road." "I was, this morning, for the mail." "Was there any?" she said. "Nothing useful. Ton of junk mail as usual. And a letter from Nina. I read it and tore it up." "You didn't." "I didn't," and pulled it from his back pocket and gave it to her. "That was unfair, holding it from me this long." "I got disoriented. Distracted, I mean, or involved in something—that's it. Came back, had read it on the way back—there's absolutely nothing new in it, by the way. Jeremy Junior's fine, hiccuping more often, that's all. Jeremy's busy at work and thought he was getting the flu. Sunny weather, stormy weather, a film dealing with values and serious moral questions that we also might want to see on VCR, and her book's going well. But then I saw the cellar doors, opened them because I thought of painting the chair. Now I'm finished," and put the brush down. "One thing we can use down here is running water so I can clean my brushes and hands, though not at the expense of converting this dungeon into a shaped-up basement. Bringing down a pail of water and leaving the liquid soap here does the trick just as well." He cleaned the brush, then his hands, dried everything on his pants. "Maybe a paper-towel roll would help too, but not a rack for it please. The pail was from a few days ago, if you're wondering." "I'm not," she said, reading the letter. "Is what she says in it any different than what I said? I tend to miss things, and not read between lines. Oh, this is getting us nowhere. Let's go upstairs." "What's getting us nowhere?" she said. "I don't know. I just said it to get us out of here," and he shut the light.

He grabbed her elbow and moved her to the steps. They went up them, she holding onto his arm till she was able to grab the edge of one of the folded-up cellar doors. When they reached the top, a bird swooped down on them. "Duck," he said, pushing her head down till she was on her knees with him. The bird came a few inches from hitting them. "That crow was aiming at us," he said. "Where's my gun?" "You have no gun," she said. "I don't, huh?" He pointed his finger at the crow, which was circling about fifty feet up, followed its movements with his finger for a while, then

said "Bang-bang, you're dead, you bum." The crow's wings col-
lapsed, and it dropped to the ground some twenty feet from them.
"I don't believe it. Did you see that?" "I saw it," she said, "and I
don't believe it either." "With this gun," holding up his finger. "Do
you think if I pointed it your way and said bang-bang, I'd knock
you off too?" "Why, you want to? Anyway, don't try." "But it's ridiculous. Just by going bang-bang, I killed that bird. And I had a
bead on him too. 'Bead' is the word they use for it—out West or in
criminal or law-enforcement circles—right?" "You're asking me?"
"Bead, a bead, or maybe it's 'draw a bead,' but like you're aiming."
"The beads I know are little stones and ornaments around the
neck and droplets and so on. Of sweat. I still can't believe what you
did though." "Neither can I. I aimed my finger at it—like this,"
and he pointed his finger at her, "and then when it seemed to be
closest to me and my hand wasn't shaking so much, I fired. Bang-
bang. I didn't pull any trigger, though, meaning, use another finger as if I were pulling one." He still had his finger on her. "Maybe
I should move it away from you just to be safe." "Don't be silly. We
both are. It was a coincidence. The crow died of a heart attack, but
not one brought on by you, or something like that when you pre-
tended to shoot it. Pull it if you want. Shoot it. Go bang-bang, even
bang-bang-bang. Three shots for the price of two. Suddenly today
I'm feeling very brave." "Bang-bang," he said. Her face got dis-
torted, hands sort of stiffened into claws, and she fell to the
ground. "Darling," he said and got on his knees. Her eyes were
closed. She was on her side, and he put his ear to her chest, moved
it around above her breasts, her back about where he thought her
heart would be behind, then her nose and mouth. He didn't hear
or feel anything. He did it again: chest, back, nose and mouth, and
then put his mouth on hers, kept her mouth open with his hands,
and breathed into it, took his mouth away, took in a mouthful of
air, breathed into her again, pulled away. "Oh Christ, what have I
done? What have I done, goddamnit?" he screamed out. He stood,
forced his fist into his palm, screamed "What the hell have I done?
I've killed my wife. It can't be so." Got on the ground, listened to
her chest, mouth, put his hand on her neck where he thought her
pulse might be, was none, felt around her neck and temples, didn't
try her wrist because he was never able to find it there, turned her
over on her stomach, straddled her, did what he thought was the

thing to do to get someone breathing again. Pushed down with his hands, sat up, pushed, sat up. Lay down next to her and put his ear to her mouth; turned her over and put his ear where he thought her heart was. Nothing. He pointed his finger and pressed it into his forehead. "Bang-bang," he said. "Bang-bang. Bang-bang." I'm not shot, he thought. Not even hurt. "Come on, sweetheart, you got to be kidding." He sat her up, held her while he listened to where he thought her heart was. Thought he heard something. Touched her neck. He felt something. Forced her eyes open. They looked alive. She smiled. "*You*," he said, "you nearly gave me a heart attack there." "You'd kill yourself for me? I peeked. Oh my dearest," and she hugged him. "Yes I would," he said. "I was so full of guilt and everything else. Sadness. I suddenly believed . . . well, who wouldn't after he shot that bird down? The bird," and he stood up, helped her up and ran to where the crow had landed.

It was still there. "I don't want to put my head near its heart or beak, for those things can bite. No wonder I hit it. Look at its size." "Kick it," she said, walking over. "You mean nudge it with my foot. Okay. But if it jumps it's going to startle me." He touched it with the tip of his shoe, then jabbed it. The crow moved but didn't seem alive. "Think it's alive but just pretending?" he said. "I wouldn't doubt it. —Seriously," she said, "I don't think so. I think it got that heart attack or the cerebral equal of one—a flying stroke or something winged animals get only when they're flying, and not particularly when people below are shooting their fingers at them, but that's all. Your bang-bang and its fatal heart failure or stroke are only coincidental, one chance in a million, and it came up today." "I hope so. Because I wouldn't want to personally kill anything living like that. But come on, crow," he said to the bird, "move, move, get up, fly or walk away. Do your messy garbage-bag biting and picking, your squawking, keeping us up when we want to take afternoon naps or sleep late. Do what the hell you're supposed to and don't make me feel bad, because the one-in-a-million coincidence I can't prove."

The crow began fidgeting, stood up—they backed away— flapped its wings, seemed to be testing its feet out on the ground, flapped some more, tried to fly, looked at them, walked backward away from them a few feet, flapped harder while it walked front- ward even farther away from them and took off, flew a few inches off the ground several yards, then up to the sky. He pointed his finger at it, held his wrist while he got a bead on it. She said "Don't chance it; not today. Maybe you did kill it and then your little entreaty before brought it back to life, and you won't be so fortunate the next time." He said "Just a test to prove my supernatural or whatever-you-want-to-call-them powers—powers I never had that I know of but am now naturally curious to see if I do. —Hold it. Steady, steady. I've got it. Bang-bang. And bang, just in case." The crow flew on, settled in a tree. "Maybe I missed." "Or you wounded it," she said. "Well, I'm not going to find out. In fact, no more games or tests like that. In fact, I'm throwing away my gun," and flicked his hand to the side. They heard a clump in the grass about ten feet away in the direction he'd flicked to. "You believe that?" "It must be a rabbit or squirrel," she said, "or a mouse." "Probably a mouse." "But then again, who knows? Though we should try to find out."

She went over to where they'd heard the clump. Nothing moved. "Maybe it's already gone," she said. "Or it could have been something that just went down a hole, didn't need to go through the grass. But we won't tell anybody about all this, okay?" "I don't know," he said. "It's a good story to tell, raises lots of interesting questions, puts what you didn't think you thought right out there, right? And we're having dinner with the Chamberlains later and they're so dull that they're wonderful to shock, so why not?" "It might be somewhat off-putting to them. They'll think we're getting loony and they'll tell people, and then everyone will think we've become peculiar." "Let them," he said. "If they don't like it, let them ostracize us too. Then we won't have to return the dinner invitation to the Chamberlains and all our other dull neighbors who sort of force us to socialize more than we like. Let the whole town know, for all I care. It'll give us more time to ourselves and what we really like to do. Like reading, for God's sake. I'm going in to read. Like a good cup of hot tea, or a drink?" "I'll make it for you," she said. "No, it was my suggestion, and what I want to do, and you put up and will probably still have to put up with all my antics today, so I'll make it for you."

A crow in the tree that their crow flew in crowed. "It doesn't necessarily have to be the one you shot at," she said. "That's a favorite resting and gabbing place of theirs," he said. "In fact—I just figured it out—I bet it's nesting there, or protecting a nest of another crow there. That's why it swooped down on us. Because I've never seen one so aggressive, except with dogs and cats." "It could be sick," she said, "distemper, or whatever crows get." "No, it looked too healthy on the ground. Children, wonderful, just what we need around here, more crows. But I like the idea of an animal protecting its young or soon-to-be young or someone else's." A crow crowed from the tree. "See, it agrees with me. We won't tell the Chamberlains this part, because it's getting too silly. But this, yes," and he aimed his finger at the tree and said "Bang-bang-bang, bang-bang, bang, bang, bang-bang," moving his finger around to different places in the tree. He imagined several crows dropping out. "Ah, wonderful, a longer sleep tomorrow morning, maybe even after that a caw-free afternoon nap. Actually, I'm glad I didn't hit any. Some of them might have been young. Let's go in before we truly get silly." "Did we shut off the cellar light?" she said. "I don't remember. I'll see you inside. Put up the water, or take out the ice tray," and he headed for the cellar. A crow crowed from the tree. "That a boy," he said, "or that a girl. Whatever you are, crow, crow." What I'd like to know, he thought, peering into the cellar and seeing it was dark, is why I didn't hear her breathing or feel her neck pulse or her heartbeat when I checked. The pulse, even in the neck, can be a little difficult to find, and I was nervous. Even her heartbeat, but her breath? He flipped the cellar doors closed with his feet. They made a loud double bang, and she yelled from kitchen window "What's that?" "Just closing things up," he said, "and the light was out. You do it? Because I don't remember I did," and he went inside.

VOICES, THOUGHTS

Gordon hears voices in his head again today. They tell him don't go out, stay in, don't bother to make lunch, have a snack, say something nice to your wife next time you see her, don't be a fake, make sure to give your kids a kiss when you pick them up and ask them what they did, where're you going? what're you doing? stay put, get up, run in place a bit, don't budge, read, nap, think about things, think about Louise.

He thinks about Louise. She was very young when he first knew her, they both were, three, four, five years old. They played together for years. Her house, his. She once let him see her with her panties down. People said they were like husband and wife sometimes. That they were sure to marry each other when they grew up. "Do you want to?" they asked and he said yes. "Do you want to?" they asked her and she said "I don't know, I think so, it's not something you can just say, maybe yes." He took her to his basement. That was one of the places they played. He said he'd give her something, he forgets what, no doubt something he thought valuable and which she would too, and she said "Don't tell, don't ever tell or I'll never play with you again," and showed, let his eyes stay on it for a few seconds from a few feet away, and when he stuck his hand out to touch, he wasn't going to go further, he didn't know there was anything further, she said "Don't be a pig," and pulled her panties up and dropped her dress over them. They continued to play together a few more years, but less and then much less. She had her girl friends, he had his friends, all boys. He last saw her when she was around ten. They'd been going to different schools for a couple of years, she to a parochial one, he to a public. She moved off the block. He didn't know she had till she was gone. That was it, never saw or heard from her or anything about her again.

Think about Willy. His wife passes and says "Really none of my business, but aren't you going to move from that chair today?" and he says "It's Sunday, day of resting, and kids are out, so what's the difference? Besides, I'm thinking," and she says "Of what?" and he says "Just thinking; I don't want to break it, so I'll tell you later." Willy was his best friend for years. Soon after he first met Willy, Gordon said if he wanted he'd teach him how to box. Gordon thought himself a pretty good boxer. An uncle had given him two pairs of gloves and a mouthpiece and he used to practice in front of his mirror in his undershorts and sometimes punch his pillow across the room. They went to the basement and put the gloves on—he forgets how they were able to tie the last glove; probably Gordon, feeling he had the advantage, left one of his gloves untied and the one he was able to tie he did with one hand and his teeth— and he showed him how to jab, punch, feint, dance, block a punch, keep the face and neck covered, what going below the belt meant, and after a while Willy said "No more, I give up, my face hurts, I'll never get the hang of it." A few months later Willy asked for a rematch and Gordon thought this was a good chance to try out the fancy footwork and bolo punch he saw in a movie newsreel of a recent champion middleweight fight, and they went to the basement and Willy outboxed him from the start. Willy hurt his nose—he was about two inches taller and ten pounds heavier and had a much longer reach than him and was now wearing his own mouthpiece—made his lips bleed, punched him silly and danced around and ducked in a way that Gordon, after the first of what were going to be three two-minute rounds, ended up swinging wildly and a couple of times landing on the floor. He never said to Willy "You beat me good, how the hell you learn all that so fast and where'd you get the mouthpiece?" He just stepped back, spit out his mouthpiece and took off his gloves and said "I'm bushed, been feeling weak for days; let's go out and play." They never boxed again, never fought, except for a few quick arguments, in any kind of way. They usually walked to school together, met outside after school to walk home, spent time together weekends, did this till they graduated in the eighth grade. Then Willy went to an agricultural high school in Queens—his grandfather owned a farm near Hartford and said he'd give him half of it—and Gordon to a special academic one in Brooklyn, and they didn't see each other much for a year, and then not at all unless they bumped into each other on the subway going or coming home from school or on the block or in a neighborhood store or movie theater, let's say. Then Willy's dad got a super's job in an apartment building on the East Side, and Gordon never saw Willy again till about twenty years later when Willy was at their favorite Central Park West corner watching spot with his kids for the Macy's Thanksgiving Day parade and Gordon was back with his folks till he got his own place. Willy introduced his girls to him—"This little pip-squeak was one of your daddy's friends when he lived here." He said what he did—a printer upstate—and then the parade started and Willy pushed his kids closer to the police barricades and then under them so they could all sit on the street, and when it was over Gordon thought he'd talk some more with him over coffee and juice and English muffins or something for his kids at the Cherry Restaurant on Columbus, but couldn't find him.

Think of Rachel. Thinks. Standing up in front of her third-story window, and the boys shouting "Take off your clothes, Rachel"—older boys first, then the younger ones joining in— "Take off all your clothes and show us," and she disappeared and came back without her clothes on—he'd been told she'd done this before—and they all whistled and cheered and an older boy yelled "Put one finger in your mouth, Rachel, and now the other in your peepee hole," and she did this and they whistled and cheered. Then her mother came to the window, pulled Rachel in, opened the window wider and shouted "You bad boys, you scum of the earth, you're the worst of the worst, ditches you should dig for yourselves and die in, picking on a poor dumb girl like this, making her do things so wicked. Go home. All of you, I know you and I'm calling your mothers, so they'll be looking for you to scold and I hope give a beating to, so run home quick, you slime, for I'm also calling the police." He was scared what his mother would say and stayed away from home till dinner time, and when he got there his mother asked what did he do to Rachel? "Nothing, she was up in her window when I last saw her when I was walking up the block, so what could I have done to her?" and she said "Did you encourage her to do what her mother said you did?—the gang of you, Ben, Willy, Caesar and whatever other morons you have out there, though Willy I'm surprised," and he said "I had nothing to do with anything, the older boys were the ones who said for her to do what she did, and I just stayed there because they'd stopped and I was walking to the park with them." She believed him but told him to walk away from things like that from now on and docked him a week's allowance. His father heard about it later and said he was lying and raised his hand as if to hit him and sent him to bed right after supper and took away his allowance for the next four weeks and barred him from spending any of the money he made on his own. Rachel's parents took her out of kindergarten and from first grade on sent her by bus—"At a tremendous expense to them too, which they can't afford," his mother said—to a religious elementary and then high school.

"So come on, out with it, what are you thinking about so deeply?" his wife says, going upstairs, which means she had come downstairs and passed him twice without him even knowing it. "Though of course if you don't want to talk about it, that's okay too," and he says "Just some things, decisions, worries—let me first think them through a little more before I talk about them. But lots of things are troubling me, you can probably see that just from the strained look on my face," and she says "No, you look all right, not smiling but not in any grieved or harried state." "Well that's good, but it's for sure not how I've been feeling, for I've had thoughts running through like mortality, growing possibilities of sickness, painful illness, lots of nice things to look forward to— goddamn teeth every third week it seems with new problems, not to mention the daily reports of a collapsing globe, and my work, or lack of much satisfaction and completion in it. Kids growing up and leaving home and what they ultimately have to face, though who knows? Maybe they'll do much better at it than I. And some of the terrible things I've done to them—you know, we've spoken of it—my anger, outbursts, pushing them hard, physically a few times, once slapping Sylvia's face, ranting at them a couple of times that I wish they'd never been born or I was dead—that I find very difficult to live with. Well, not as bad as that, and the 'live with' and 'was dead' must sound funny, but also some deeper philo-sophical questions if some of those weren't," and she says "Like what? I've got time," and he says "Nothing I can really talk about clearly right now—those are just floating around; but I'll nab the buggers and get back to you with them later, I swear," and she says "Good, I'll be interested," and throws him a kiss and goes upstairs.

Think about Thomas. Thomas was a new kid on the block, they quickly became friends, for a while they also used to meet almost every weekday morning and then pick up Willy in front of his building and all walk to school. Then one day Thomas wasn't out-side his building waiting for him and wasn't in school that day and wasn't outside his building or in school the next day and Gordon asked his mother if he could call him and did. "Thomas is ill and won't be returning to school this whole year," Thomas's mother said, "thank you for calling," and he said "Does that mean after the summer too, since it's only April now?" and she said "No, he could be back sometime in the fall, though thank you for calling, Thomas will appreciate it," and she hung up before he could say "Can I please speak to him if he's not too sick and it's okay?" He told his mother he wanted to talk to Thomas to say he hopes he'll feel better, and she said "Possibly she didn't realize that, I think it'd be all right to call again." He did, asked Thomas's mother if he could visit him—"I could do it right now, I'm just a few houses up the block"—and she said "Oh no, my dear, he's much too out of sorts to see anyone now. Maybe in a month or so, probably more like two," and he said "Like in June? I hope not July because then I'll be away in camp for two months," and she said "If we're lucky, the end of June. But don't you worry about him, he'll be better soon enough and will be delighted you called." Almost every time he passed Thomas's building the next few weeks he looked up to the fourth-floor brownstone window where his bedroom was, hoping to see him and wave. A few times he thought he should yell up to him "Thomas, it's me, Gordon, can you come to the window—is there anything you want—are you okay?" but never did. His mother bought a get-well card for him to sign and leave above Thomas's mailbox, the class sent him a card they all signed, and he called him once more to see how he was—maybe even get him to the phone, since it seemed to have been long enough—and Thomas's mother said "He's feeling a little better, not well enough to come to the phone though, but I will tell him you called—he's loved all the attention he's received lately from his teachers and friends." About two weeks later his mother said she had some very bad news to tell him and he thought "Did I do something bad I don't know about? Are they planning to move from the city and take me away from all my friends? Is one of my uncles or aunts very sick or did one of them die?" Two of them already had, one on a golf course, the other in a bathroom, and this is how she started to tell him it. She said "Your friend Thomas died two days ago in the hospital—that's where he's mostly been the last few weeks," and he said "Well not two weeks ago, because that's when I talked to his mother and she said he was home." "Maybe she was keeping it from you, knowing how you'd feel. He had a weak heart, something he was born with, and it simply wouldn't work for him anymore." She was going to the funeral, he said he wanted to, and she said it was during school hours and, besides, he was much too young to go to a young person's funeral. "They're much sadder than an adult's, and it might be upsetting for the boy's parents to see you there." He thought it strange she wanted to go; she hardly knew Thomas, didn't even seem to like him when he was over at the house, but he went along with how she explained it: Since he couldn't go, it was her way of showing his feelings and the family's respects. Later that day after the funeral he asked how it was and she said there was a good turnout, she'd never seen such an array of flowers in the chapel, the coffin was open, which she didn't think was right, till the ceremony began. "I'm glad I stopped you from going. It was the first funeral of a child I've been to and was almost too sad for me to take." He asked if any kids were there and she said "Cousins, I heard, your age and younger, which is all right I suppose if they were close, but nobody from your class." Just about everytime he walked past Thomas's building the next few weeks he looked at his window. The shade was always down and then one day it was up and the next day there were Venetian blinds on it. Sometimes, the next few years, he saw Thomas's parents in the neighborhood or on the block, together or alone, and they always asked how he was and to give their regards to his parents, whom they'd barely met and probably not his father once, and a few times said he was getting tall and seemed to be sprouting a little hair above his lips and was growing up to be a fine handsome young man and asked how school was and Miss O'Brien, his and Thomas's former teacher. Please give her their regards too. He still, when he visits his mother, occasionally bumps into Mr. Neuman, Thomas's father, who never recognizes him till he points out who he is: "Gordon Mandelbaum from up the block, number twenty-three, my dad's the druggist at La Rochelle." Mrs. Neuman died about five years after Thomas. "Heartbreak over her son," his mother said. "It had to be that, for just by her looks and build and the type of work she did for a living till that time, I didn't think there was a healthier woman alive."

"Gordon," his wife yells downstairs from the bedroom, he thinks, and he says "Yeah?" and she says "If you'd like to pay me a visit, this might be a good time," and he says "Why not," looks at the clock, has about an hour before he has to pick up the kids, "I'll be up soon," and she says "If it's any problem—I don't want to push you—don't bother; I've plenty of work to do too," and he says "No, just that I'm this moment involved in something; give me a few minutes," and she says "I'll be here."

Thinks of Vera. He once said something, he forgets what, something about she was skinny, and she grabbed him in a headlock, threw him to the ground—how old could he have been: eight, nine?—sat on top of his chest and slapped his face and said "Don't ever call me that again." His cheek stung, he thought maybe he could buck her off him; if he hadn't doubled over laughing like a jerk right after he'd said it, she never could have got his arms around his head and thrown him. How come none of his friends or hers don't jump in and stop her or tell her to get off? She held her hand out flat and said "You want it again? So say you won't say what I said for you not to," and he said "I'm sorry, I don't fight with girls so I'm not fighting back," and she said "You're not fighting back because you know I'd lick you to kingdom come," and he thought "lick," he'd heard how some of the older boys used it, he ought to too with her but that might make her madder and she had him on his back, where, if he couldn't buck her off, she could really hurt him bad before he got up, slapping again, pulling his hair and kicking him in the nuts when he was starting to get up. She was taller and older, but he hadn't thought she was as strong as she showed. He said "I just don't fight with girls, and you're not a better fighter than me, but let me up, I think you already tore my pants, and my mom's going to kill me," for now one of his knees hurt as if it had got scraped through the pants. "If anyone tore your clothes, you did it to yourself for what you said to me, you anus," and she got off him. He stood up, looked at his friends, one staring seriously at him, other two laughing, probably at what she just called him, he said "She thinks she's so tough with"—he was going to say "her big filthy trap"—"but she isn't," and walked away, didn't look at his pants till he was in his building's vestibule, thought why'd she call him an anus? He thinks he knows what it is but what's it got to do with everything else that happened and all she did? His pants were ripped in a way where he knew his mother couldn't just sew them, they'd have to be taken to the tailor to weave and that cost a fortune. He washed his knee, put some hydrogen peroxide and a Band-Aid on the cut, changed into another pair of pants, and brought the ripped ones to his mother and said he tore them and put his finger in the hole. She said "How?" and he said he was playing statues on a stoop, "I know it was a stupid thing to do and I won't do it again, but I fell off it to the sidewalk when I had one foot up and the person who was 'it' told us to freeze." Sometime later Vera was wearing a skirt and socks and a friend of his said someone had told him she had no underpants on and was completely naked underneath and that she also had hair there, "a little of it, like a Hitler mustache, but some." "How's he know?" and his friend said "Because he was behind her in their building when she was walking up a steep flight of stairs today and she bent over for something, maybe just to show him, and he saw it. Let's pretend we're fighting, you get me on the ground or me you, we'll roll her way and under her skirt and see," and he said "Suppose she sees us and minds?" and his friend said "She won't know, we'll be fighting and rolling and not paying any attention to her, our eyes looking like we hate each other till we get underneath her skirt." They did that. "You little pimp." "You little dick," the words were all rehearsed, grabbed each other, fell to the ground, started rolling her way. "What do you think you're doing?" she said, they continued rolling, she jumped aside, they changed directions and rolled together where she now was. She said "You're both asking for it if you don't stop." They couldn't because they were rolling too hard now, and she kicked him in the head and his friend in the back but probably had aimed at his head. He didn't know what kind of shoe she had on, but it made a gash in his head. He was bleeding all over the place, someone offered him a dirty hanky to stop it, somebody else some bunched-up tissues, he held the tissues to the cut and went home and into the bathroom and put a towel to it. His mother came in and said "Oh my God," and he said "Don't worry, Mom, I was running down the block and tripped and hit my head against a streetlight but I'll be all right, it's already starting to stop." She called his uncle, who was a doctor in Washington Heights, and his uncle said it didn't sound bad enough to drive down for—he wasn't unconscious, not even dizzy, and the blood didn't seem to be gushing— just press some sterile gauze to it till the bleeding stops, then ice and later antiseptic on it and if it seems more than a superficial cut and doesn't stop bleeding in about fifteen minutes, he'll drive down and sew it up. It didn't stop for half an hour, but he didn't want any needles and thread in his head so told his mother not to call his uncle back. About a year later Vera's dad got a good job in an Ohio factory, and they moved out there.

Feels the scar from the kick, thinks of Horace. Horace was a little kid, about three, standing behind him in the middle of the street when he swung a broomstick at a ball in a stickball game and hit him in the head. Horace went down, he thought he'd killed him, his eyes were closed and he didn't move except for a little hand-wiggling, some boys ran under Horace's windows and yelled "Mrs. Rich, Mrs. Rich, Gordon hit Horace's head with a stick and he's bleeding badly, he might be dead." She stuck her head out the window, a car was coming down the street and the boys flagged it down. A man got out and said "I'm a fireman, I know how to take care of things like this." Other cars were honking behind his. "Lift the kid to the sidewalk so we can pass," one driver yelled. Mrs. Rich was screaming from her window, then yelled at the fireman

"Don't touch him, nobody move him, back up if you got to go any-place, I'll be right down." She was a big strong woman with a tough mouth, and Gordon thought she'd grab him and swing him around and then slap the hell out of him. She went straight to Horace, listened for his breathing, said to Gordon "Run to your father in the pharmacy and have him give you some boxes of cotton and bandages and also to call Roosevelt for an ambulance, I already did." The fireman opened Horace's eyes, looked at them and let them close. "They're starting to move normally," he said, "he'll be okay." Police and an ambulance were there, and Horace was sobbing by the time Gordon got back with the cotton and bandages, Gordon's dad called the hospital that night and was told Horace had gone home, he called Mrs. Rich and she said no bones broken, no concussion, just a deep crack in his forehead that took twelve stitches to close. "If you have no objections, Doc, and from someone who's been a good customer of yours too, I'd like to send you the hospital bill." He said "If it's a lot and I'm not covered, maybe we can split it half and half, because though Gordon should have looked around before he got up to swing, your son shouldn't have been so close to home plate," then put on Gordon, who apologized as he'd been told to. He saw Mrs. Rich about a week later coming home from shopping, waved in an embarrassed way and wanted to quickly pass her or cross the street but she said she'd like to speak to him. He went over to her, thinking she might drop her bags and maybe smack him. She said "I know how you still feel bad, I would too, since Horace still gets terrific pains in his head and has trouble with his eyes seeing. But I'm not blaming you for what you did; kids aren't smart your age and accidents happen." If she had got angry he was ready to say what his father had said to his mom, that what was a three-year-old kid doing in the street without any adult supervision? He felt awful every time after that when he saw Horace with this big bandage and then an ugly scar on his forehead and later on glasses, with the scar getting smaller and smaller it seemed, though he didn't know and never asked anyone if the accident could have had anything to do with the glasses. Then Mrs. Rich got married and they moved away, and he only thought of Horace maybe every couple of years and usually when he crossed the street near the manhole cover where that home plate was.

"Hello down there," his wife says, "are you coming up or should I forget it?" and he says "No, I'm coming," and gets out of the chair, something in him says wait, sit, just another minute, for Lillian, thinks, blue hair, black eyes, he means long black hair and very bright blue eyes, sweet face, lanky frame, ears seemed to be pinned back and were pointy, almost no nose, sits, looks at the clock, has time, studying to be a dancer and, with her hair, clothes and walk, already looked like one. When he was around twelve he wrote her a note and slipped it to her in an envelope, which said he wanted to go out with her, maybe to a Saturday or Sunday afternoon movie or something if she didn't have dance lessons then and she wrote him a note back, a girl friend of hers handed it to him in gym, that said "I'm too young and you are too and I have a lot of school to go to, let's only be friends like we've been, but thank you, kind sir," when what he really wanted to do was kiss her in the movie house as they'd done once somewhere else, maybe a date or two later hold her hand and, if he was lucky sometime after that, feel her a little bit on top through her blouse, though she only seemed to have started getting breasts, maybe much later get her to touch his dick through his pants and then outside them someplace and maybe where he could get her to hold it and later shake it till it sprayed and where he could also get to feel her bush if she had one and finger her, for that was what boys his age or a little older said they were starting to do with girls or trying to. Some months before at a birthday party, he kissed her. A couple of the other boys did too, and kissed some of the other girls, though he only got to kiss one, but he didn't know if they'd done it as hard to her and got as hard a kiss back. They were playing a type of musical chairs in which the one running around when the music was going had to sit on the lap of the person he was standing beside the second the music stopped and kiss her on the lips or, if it was a boy whose lap he sat on, shake his hand, and same thing for the girl running around but instead of shaking hands she hugged the other girl. The music stopped when he was a person away from her, but he made believe by sneaking up a few inches past the boy that he'd stopped in front of her, and he sat on her lap and she said "No fair," and everyone else it seemed said "Go ahead," and she said "Okay, but it has to be quick," and they kissed. Her mouth was slightly open when they did, his closed. He'd never kissed an open mouth and started to open his because he thought she wanted him to but she pulled away and said "That's enough, I've done it even if you cheated," and pushed him off. After that, just about whenever he saw her in school he imagined kissing her with their mouths open and feeling her up and unhooking her bra and shoving his hand down her panties and going to this special spot in Central Park behind some bushes and rocks near the bridle path where he knew some really older boys went with their girls and getting her on her back, it'd have to be warm out and not right after a rain, and sticking his prick in her, maybe with only pushing their clothes up and down but not taking anything off except the shoes, and then burying the scumbag or just tossing it under the bushes, where he and his friends had found a few used ones but mostly just the rings of them. When he came back from camp that summer he learned she'd moved to some other part of the city and wouldn't be going back to the same school for eighth grade. He wrote her a letter in care of the school, to be forwarded, held on to it for weeks before he dumped it; he just didn't think she'd be interested and he didn't want to get a letter back saying she wasn't or get no letter back and then one day bump into her or that friend of hers in school who he sometimes bumps into and be embarrassed he sent it. In it he said "If you think we're any older now, I mean from when I asked you this once, and you have some extra free time from your dance lessons and schoolwork, I'd still like going to an afternoon movie or anything you'd like with you. I hope to hear from you soon, and I hope you like your new school and life. Yours sincerely," and his first name, with his full name printed underneath, and phone number and address.

He goes upstairs. His wife's typing at her desk and he says "I'm ready but maybe I took too long and you're no longer interested," and she says "Why do you say that?" and he says "Oh, nothing; you know me by now; I can never accept good things gracefully," and she says "That's better," and gets up, he takes off his clothes, she leaves on her panties and bra and they sit on the bed. She likes him to undress her, he thinks, at least the last part, even her watch, which he takes off her wrist and then puts his arms around her, kisses her while unhitching her, and she shakes the straps off and lets the bra drop to the floor, he feels her breasts, she makes some sounds, they lie back and he puts his hand down her panties—now it's "put," now it's "slide," then it was "shove," which was probably accurate for the way he did it then or rather would have liked to and then started to a couple of years later—pushes her panties off with her help and thinks of Lillian while their eyes are closed and they're kissing and playing with each other. He didn't mean for her to come back again, "again" meaning now, and quickly opens and shuts and opens and shuts his eyes, a trick he uses to get rid of images he doesn't want, but she's still there, walking away from him down a busy street, turning around to wave at a passing car, hugging a stack of books to her chest as she leaves school, lying back with her clothes on and holding her arms up to him. Let her stay till she goes away, it won't hurt things and might even help if he can get her clothes off and see what's underneath. Then she becomes skinny Mark, body and face, in his old woolen clothes and long wavy hair when the rest of them at that age—eleven, twelve, late spring when he first met him—were wearing shorts and had something bordering on the crew cut, and he blinks repeatedly till Mark disappears. He came over from Europe after the war, lived with his sister and aunt in a Columbus Avenue tenement across from their side street; the rest of his family died in the camps. He thinks he remembers him saying he and his sister survived by his nanny passing them off as Poles. He learned English fast, soon got great grades, skipped out of Gordon's class but they still stayed friends, got into a special academic high school and moved away, but that was later on. Gordon couldn't teach him baseball or football or anything like that; his game was soccer and he did fantastic tricks with a basketball with his feet, chest, knees, head, back of his neck. He showed up on the block a year after he left, looking for Gordon; they talked, nothing was foreign about him anymore, not even his speech, and that was the last time he saw him. Did he take down Mark's phone number and address? Doesn't think so. Did he expect old friends to always contact him? Doesn't remember if he had that attitude then. Now, since he likes working at home and doesn't much like going out for very long or having people over, he hardly sees anyone but his children and wife. "Mark my words about Mark," one of their teachers said several times, "he'll be a great mathematician or physicist or something like that in the sciences, which might not seem like much to those of you who don't even know what a physicist is. But mark my words, twenty years from now you'll see his face and what he's doing in the news-papers and you'll recognize his name." He wonders what Mark became or just what became of him, has stopped kissing and feeling.

"Something the matter?" his wife says, and he says "Oh, you know, just that heady all-consuming philosophical thinking push-ing in again," and she says "So tell me, I can stop to listen, seeing how you've stopped," and he says " 'To listen'—that's right, that's what it is and why I stopped—no, I don't know what I'm talking about, and all that baloney before about my having deep and de-manding philosophical thoughts and also thoughts of big deci-sions and worries and remorse over how I'm treating the kids and the growing possibilities of disabling and painful illnesses—my teeth, I remember—well, they were all just that, baloney, is what I'm saying," and she says "Why? How?" and rests her head on his thigh, and he says "What I mean is, it's just not like me or in me to think philosophically—I mostly just go on and on and don't stop to think, so I was evading your questions from not now but before, and of course also now, meaning just before," and she says "Wait, I'm losing you," and he says "I'm saying that if I do get a philo-sophical thought it's usually by accident—I'm thinking of some-thing practical, let's say, and the philosophical thought just pops up, but it mostly usually comes from something like, if I get a pain in my stomach that wakes me up two consecutive nights and keeps me up, I think maybe I have pancreatic cancer—the one they can't detect till it's in an untreatable stage because it was hidden behind some other organs, and that might make me think of my mortality, of how I'd hate to go so fast and leave you and the kids while they're so young and also the physical pain I'd have before they doped me up with morphine and the emotional pain it would bring the kids of their daddy dying and probably to you too," and she says "Of course me, what do you think?" and he says "I know, but you could recover after a while—a year, half a year—and marry again, while with them they've lost their father perma-nently, there's really no one to replace him if he goes when they're so young—but what was I saying? And truth is, even that wasn't a good example of a philosophical thought—it wasn't even one. So maybe I never get philosophical thoughts, or I get them only rarely but never deep ones. But I was saying or was going to say that I didn't have any philosophical thoughts before when I was sitting downstairs and told you I did, or thoughts of worry and remorse and so on, but only a rush of thoughts with pictures and scenes and the rest of it of kids I knew when I was between maybe five and fifteen. I don't even know why the thoughts came, or why those particular kids, some of whom I haven't thought of in maybe thirty years, though maybe the more erotic scenes—one was of seeing a girl's vagina for the first time when I was four or five, or first time where I remembered it—came in simply because I was feeling amorous and wanted to make love, even if it took me a while to get up here, and so those excited me to it. Anyway, they won't stop me anymore—I think enough time's elapsed where I'm done with them for now—and we better get going again since we don't have much more time," and runs his hand over her shoulder and across her mouth, and she moves her face next to his and they resume making love.

He's behind her, place he likes best, her buttocks up and his hands holding her hips, pretty close to the finish he guesses since it hardly ever takes him long when they're like this, much as he'd like to keep going for her sake, though she was the one who said "Come behind me"—probably because they were so short of time and she was nowhere near done—something he often hopes she'll suggest and he rarely initiates since she's said it's never the best position for her and she does it mostly because she knows how much he loves it. "Not that I'm saying it's horrible," she once said, "it's just that I can't see you and it's rough on my elbows and knees and the pleasure isn't the greatest so it's simply not one of my favorites," when he thinks of Bea Fields. Standing in front of an audience, hands cupped to her chest, eyes closed, face transported, moving her mouth as if singing. He liked to sing also and could tell her voice was beautiful with clean tones and a tremendous range though it seemed for her age a little artificial and too trained. Mr. Sisk, the music teacher, said a few times he'd like them to do a duet in front of the assembly, since they had the best voices in school, and he was glad it never got past an idea. She usually snubbed him, seemed to look down on all the boys, maybe because she knew how they felt about her and also because she thought they had no culture and she didn't think much of their brains. She was homely, big thick glasses, large nose, piano legs they said, messy frizzy hair, big fat breasts before it seemed any of the other girls started to get theirs or only had buds, waist and hips like those women who wore bustles in old-fashioned westerns though she was only twelve or thirteen, ugly dresses and shoes, big lips, little teeth, whiny speaking voice, it was said she never studied for tests but she always ended up with top marks, he and a few others also tried out for Performing Arts but she was the only one to get in. At their graduation ceremony she sang a Negro spiritual, something from a popular operetta and *La Bohème*, and then, other than for once or twice in the neighborhood, he never saw her again.

He comes, keeps moving as long as he can, then she lies on her stomach and he collapses on top of her. They stay that way, side of face against side of face, her eye closed, probably the other one too, and she's murmuring while he thinks of Gwynn. The best athlete for a girl he ever played with, and then she lost a leg below the knee because of some rare bone disease her first year in high school. Then she was in a wheelchair without the other leg and last time he saw her was when he was going to a movie alone, it was his first or second year in college, and she was in her chair in front of her apartment building a block from the theater, she must have been left there since it was a walk-up and she couldn't have got downstairs herself, and he said "Gwynn?" though he knew it was her, and she said "Gordon Tannenbaum, or Mandelbaum?" and he said "Mandelbaum, though no difference," and asked how she was and she said fine, doing okay, considering, she finally graduated high school with an equivalency diploma by having a slew of special-education teachers come to her home and that she was even planning to go to college, which she bet he was in now and he said he was, but also working, but that was good, her going to college, getting out and around and really exercising the brain, and he thought maybe she'd like to go to the movie with him, he could handle it, wheeling her there and back or she could do her own wheeling if that was the kind of wheelchair it was and she had the strength for it and preferred doing it, and then he'd just ring up her apartment and someone would come down for her and get her up however they do it and he'd even pay her way, treat her at the candy counter and everything, but said "Well, I'll see ya," and she said "It's been nice talking, stop by again," and he felt bad after he left, and looked back from the corner and saw her talking with an older woman but looking at him. She waved, he waved, he continued going but told himself he would stop by, maybe even phone for her to meet him downstairs or he'd come upstairs to help her down, and later heard, maybe a year after, she'd been sent to a hospital in the Midwest that specialized in her disease and that was the last he heard anything about her. He wonders if these people, the ones who didn't die, ever think of him. His wife says from under him "You better fetch the kids," and he says "Right, I forgot," looks at the clock, gets up and wipes himself and dresses and quickly leaves.

BATTERED
HEAD

He bangs his head against something when he's exercising. He sees light, feels blood, goes into the bathroom—all this was done in the dark, just a little moonlight—turns on the light there and sees the cut. "How could I have been so stupid?" he thinks. "Unfamiliar house; we were here last summer for a month but our first night in it this one; why didn't I turn on the lights?" He was exercising in the dining room, which has the stairway in it, and his daughter was sleeping or falling asleep upstairs with her door open because she was afraid to sleep with it closed and he didn't want the light to wake her. He already has a paper towel to the cut, looks at it and at the cut in the mirror, still bleeding, presses harder, thinks he should get an ice pack on it to keep down the swelling, goes into the dining room to get to the kitchen but stops to see what he banged his head on. Stands on the spot where he thinks he was exercising. Must have been one of those two spindles or stems or whatever they are—just the top poles of the back of the dinner table chair on his left, that he hit his head on. The exercise was where he puts his hands on his hips—no, clasps them behind his neck and touches his left knee with his left elbow and then his right knee with his right elbow and does that ten times. It's the first of a series of exercises he devised for himself years ago and has been doing every morning or late evening or sometimes at his office in the afternoon, if he has about ten minutes and the door's closed and he hasn't done it that morning and prefers getting it over with rather than doing it that night. He was only doing the first movement of the exercise when he banged his head. The cut seems dry, and he takes off the towel. Still bleeding, and now hurts, and he folds the towel over, presses a clean part to his head and goes to the bathroom for last year's aspirins. This year's he hasn't unpacked yet.

Next morning his daughter says "Where'd you get that?" and he says "If I told you I got it exercising last night, you'd say I must have been drunk." "Huh?" and he says "What I'm saying is I did get it exercising—doing this, which I won't be able to do for a while with this head," and shows her. "Oh Jesus, that hurt, and it's still bleeding, I see, and I wasn't drunk when I got it, sweetie. I was just unfamiliar with the terrain—this room, so what I thought was air was a chair, no po-tree intended." She says "Well it looks ugly and you should put a Band-Aid on it," and he thinks "She'll be ashamed of it if I take her to camp as is, and she'll be right."

At camp the counselor he leaves her with says "What happened there?" pointing to the Band-Aid and Mercurochrome stain around it, and he says "If I told you I banged up my head exercising, you'd say," but because his daughter's there he should change the line, "that I'm either drunk saying that or was drunk when I got it. But I'm not, wasn't not—either, neither. I got it in the most paradoxical way possible—like jogging, I mean dying of a heart attack jogging, you know what I mean?" and she nods, and he thinks she doesn't know or has stopped listening. He should know whom he's talking to, not go over or under or try to ram through their heads. And maybe his head's been affected by the blow worse than he knows.

Says good-by to his daughter, kisses her lips, says he'll be here 3:30 promptly or even a quarter hour before, "since all the campers do the last fifteen minutes is hang around in the sun waiting to be picked up. We'll stop at the Hillside View Diner for a snack on the way home. You'll have fun here, meet lots of girls. Don't forget to take sailing, if you want, as your main morning activity for the month. I want her to," he says to the counselor, "because I want her to teach me everything she learns." "And we'll try to teach her everything we know." His daughter never says a word. Didn't want to come. Said yesterday during the drive up "I'm not going to camp, just so you know." Said it a few days ago, weeks ago, in February when he was filling out the application: "You say your money's so hard-earned? Well I don't care if you waste it and I won't be guilty if you don't get a refund." She pulls her head away when he tries kissing the top. He says "Well, good-by, my dearie," and walks to the car, turns around when he gets to it. She's staring sadly at him, shoulders folded in, face saying "How can you leave me here?" Her glasses make her look even sadder. He knows the feeling. Painfully shy—they said it about him, he says it about her, but she's even more that way than he was. The counselor sees her staring, puts her arm around her and walks her over to a group of girls, all with eyeglasses, and introduces her. They each say hello to her and resume their hand-slapping counting game. The counselor has a volleyball-size ball under her arm, throws it to one of the girls; the girl catches it, looks around what to do with it and the counselor says "Toss it to Debbie—the new girl." "Here, Debbie, catch." Deborah shakes her head, steps back, looks at him. "Play, play," he mouths, and puts his hands up as if catching the ball, then throwing it forward and then from under his legs. She looks away, at no one now. Doesn't like to play ball. Thinks she's an awful athlete and clumsy runner. Likes reading books. Has always been tops in school. Likes to paint, draw, sculpt in clay, write stories and plays, make things. She has one good friend in the city; they don't even see each other that much. She's too shy to ask her over; waits till the friend asks if she can come over. He loves it when she's having fun with another kid, running around with her, laughing, confiding, sitting on the same couch reading, being wild, playing games, but it's so rare. What have we done to her? What's he done, he means, since he wanted and got custody of her.

Leaves, works at home, couple of times his head aches and he takes aspirins and rests on the bed, every so often thinks he's doing the wrong thing by forcing her to go to camp, "but then I want to work during the day so what am I supposed to do?" Intends getting back at 3:15 but wants to finish a page he worked on all day, so doesn't get there till quarter of, and the roads were clear all the way. "Sorry I'm late; traffic; one Maine driver after the other in front of me. How was it?" "My lunch was almost boiling. You left it in the sun." "Sweetheart, I left your bag in the shade behind a rock but the sun's direction must have changed. Put it where you want next time. And sailing?" "We didn't go out. Water was too choppy. Instead we played these rough games. Like red rover, which you can break your arm doing and which I think lots of them wanted to do, yours and their own. I sat out after a minute. I'm not going to make any friends or have a good time here. They all know one another from school and around. I'm the only one from the city." "There must be more. Have you checked?" "No, but I've heard. I'm not going to camp tomorrow." "You have to give it a try. I told you: after a week or so, if you still have some major grievances about it, we'll have a serious discussion about your continuing it." She sulks in the car. A counselor said good-by. A girl waved to her when they drove off. "Who was that girl who waved before?" he says. "She seemed to like you, and all the counselors too." "I don't know. She didn't swim either, so we sat next to each other at the lake." "Why didn't you swim?" "I felt cold. And there are bloodsuckers in the water." "Don't worry about those. Chances are one in a thousand one will get on you, and if it does, little touch with a cigarette or sprinkle of salt and it falls off dead." "Last summer a boy got one on his leg and it bled down to the ground." "That's the water mixing with the blood, making it seem like much more. But that girl before. Just by the way she waved, I'd say she wanted to be your friend." "You can't tell by one look. And she only talked about stupid TV shows you'd never let me watch and what a *fun time* next week's Pirate's Day is going to be. She's like most of them here and last year. They're nice but we don't like the same things." "Give them a chance. She might have brought up those shows just to—" But she's turned away, doesn't want to hear anything he says.

Next morning she screams when he tells her to get in the car to go to camp, cries when he leaves her, won't look at him when he picks her up or do anything later but complain to him at home. Same thing the next two days but worse. It's the freezing lake water, rough games, competitive sports, smelly outhouses, baby stuff they do in arts and crafts, a sort of open shed the girls have to undress in and which the boys are always peeking into, no drinking water anywhere so you have to lug around your heavy thermos everyplace or die of thirst, scavenger hunts that take hours in the woods or hot sun and turn out to mean nothing—either they disqualify half the things you find or the prize is a piece of old bubble gum.

She's sullen most of the weekend. He works a couple of hours both mornings but they do a few things after that—go to the ocean, eat in a restaurant, climb halfway up a big hill but what the locals call a mountain, pick blueberries that aren't ready yet, but he can tell that camp on Monday's usually on her mind. "All right," he says at dinner Sunday night, "list everything that's good and bad about camp, but be honest. First of all, from what I can see the girls are darn nice. One of them—Laurie or Lauren, I think—when we got to camp late Friday, ran up to you and said 'Debbie, where were you? I missed you. I thought you weren't coming today, and then you'd have missed the field trip to Goose Cove,' and took your hand and you both walked happily away." "I wasn't happy. And except for the rougher boys, it's not the kids at all." She enumerates what she hates most about camp. When she gets to "Eight, the mosquitoes, I get so many bites, I itch all day even with the scallion you rub on," he says "Listen, enough already, will you? You're just trying to fortify your argument with anything you can think against camp. Next it'll be horse flies, then poison ivy, then poisonous snakes you hear are around, though I don't think there are any in all of Maine. I'm sorry, sweetie, but after everything you've said so far, I don't buy your argument." Tears appear; "I hate you, Daddy," and she runs outside, minute later the kitchen door slams and she runs to her room. "All I'm asking," he shouts, "is for you to give it another week and then decide; what the heck's that?" Then thinks: How's he supposed to take what she said to him? She was never that harsh before. Well, just a kid her age having a tantrum, not getting what she wants, thinking he's not being completely fair, and maybe he isn't, but the hell with it. Later he'll call her in for dessert, act as if nothing happened, and she'll be fine, or almost, and probably even apologize without his prompting.

Calls her later and she doesn't come. Goes to her room. She's in bed, asleep or pretending. "Deborah, if you want to continue with the numbers where you left off, we can; I won't butt in till you're finished. I mean, no butting in; say what you want, and I'll listen and consider it seriously tonight." No response. Takes her glasses off, feels around under the covers for a book but doesn't find any, she didn't brush her teeth or get in her pajamas but he's not going to start putting them on her—hasn't for a couple of years at least—kisses her, turns the night light on and shuts off the overhead.

She gets in his bed around three. "What do you think you're doing?" "I can't sleep, and my pillow's all wet." "What are you, sweating?" "No." "Just turn it over." "Please, Dada." He doesn't like her sleeping with him but her voice is so sad, and after what happened before, so he says okay, "Tonight only, now go to sleep without another word." He gets out of bed. "Where are you going?" "The bathroom," and he takes his T-shirt and underpants with him and puts them on outside the room.

Morning, she's snuggled up to him. He gets out of bed, does his exercises in the living room, and later when he wakes her she says "Please don't send me to camp today." "Oh come on now." "Please, I only want to stay home with you, and I promise not to be a bother." "Okay, today will be the exceptional day off, but you have to leave me the entire morning free, take care of your own needs, all that stuff, and then if I want the afternoon to work to at least the time I would have left to pick you up at camp, that too." She reads, draws, sets up her easel outside and paints, swings on the swing set, jumps rope, goes down the road several times for mail and when she gets it—he sees all this through his second-floor studio window—knocks on his door. "Want me to leave your mail outside or give it to you by person?" and he says "Just leave it, sweetie, I'm in the middle of something, and thanks." Makes her lunch and sits opposite her with a coffee and yesterday's *Times*, which came in the mail today, and she says "Your cut doesn't look so ugly anymore; even if it needed a Band-Aid up to last night, you don't need one now," and he says "Yeah, seems to be healing nice, and I don't feel so dopey anymore. That's what happens when you don't do anything about it." After lunch she says "You don't have to, of course, but if you want can we go to Carter Pond to swim? I've been thinking of it all winter," and he says "Sure, I've done enough already, two pages, and I haven't swum since we got here."

Swim, diner for fish burgers, play checkers that night. Later: "What do you want for lunch tomorrow?" and she says "When I'm ready to eat it, I'll tell you." "I mean for camp." "Dada, I'm not going to camp." "You're going, now don't give me another argument. We took off one day, it was very nice, but not two." "You can't make me," and he says "Oh, I'll make you, all right. And I'll prepare whatever I want you to have for lunch, if you're not going to help me, now get ready for bed." When he comes into her room for a mosquito check and to say good night, she says "A story?" He says, looking at something on the wall he thinks is a mosquito but turns out to be the head of a nail, "No story, nothing for you tonight, just go to sleep," checks some more and turns off the light.

She tries to get in his bed early that morning. "No; you're not going to camp, you don't sleep in my bed." She goes back to her room. Wrong thing to say, he thinks, and wrongly worded. He doesn't want her in his bed, period. That wouldn't be how to say it either. How then? "Listen, you sleep in your bed, I sleep in mine, that's the way life is." No. Just: "We sleep in our own beds, period." Maybe he'll come up with something better later, or maybe he won't have to, for she might not try again.

At eight he goes to her room to wake her. "Deborah, Deborah dear," but she pretends to be asleep. He knows she's pretending. She had plenty of sleep last night, and she's a light sleeper. Feels her forehead. She's okay. Raises the shade, opens the window more, "Rise and shine, sweetheart," shakes her shoulder. She opens her eyes. "I'm not going, you can't force me." "Then I'll have to dress you and drag you there." No, wrong move and words again, and she's crying. "Okay, don't go, what the hell do I care? But don't bother me till three. You know how to read time?" "You know I do. You don't have to act sarcastic." "Good. Then don't bother me till then." "Why would I want to?"

She makes herself breakfast and lunch and a snack. He can tell by the sounds in the kitchen, dishes left in the wash pan and food spills on the tablecloth. She reads and plays in the living room and behind the house. They bump into each other a couple of times when he comes downstairs for coffee or to go to the bathroom, and he says "So how's it going?" and she says "Fine, why?" and he says "I'm glad," and quickly finishes or does what he came down for and goes upstairs. Later he's at his desk typing and sees her in her garden, her mother's sun hat on. His ex-wife left it in one of the houses they rented for the summer around here—last time they were together for a summer and when Deborah was three—and he carried it with him from house to house since, along with her duck boots and garden tools. Hair flows over her shoulders, like her mother's did and same color, and it'll be bleached the same color by the sun. She looks so beautiful and busy. Is so beautiful. Really, she doesn't want to go to camp—seems to be occupying herself okay—he shouldn't force her. Why break her will or try to? He should be subtly encouraging her to strengthen it. That the right wording? She's a shy kid, most of the time meek, and he wants her stronger, standing up to people—himself, everyone—when she thinks she's right and even when she only sort of thinks she is, but to keep an open mind while she's doing it. That's so hackneyed, he knows it, but what's the use of a more original way of saying it? What's important is what he means. Force her to go, it'll be like raping her, then, with her will busted, she'll let herself get raped again and again. Maybe it could turn out like that. And raping her mind, he means, and why that word? Because it's strong. He has no sexual feelings for her, though feels deeply for her in every other way. Parentally, the rest. Feels like crying. In the throat, a feeling she must have had first day he left her at camp, probably the other days too. His for his love for her, hers for what? Deserted, hurt, and that if he loves her, why's he doing this? On one knee now, digging, maybe weeding or replanting, garden started for her by the owner before they came up. Hell with his work—he should be spending more time with her here, little to a lot, and giving in to her more. What's his work mean anyway in comparison to her? Can't be compared, but he can find time to do it when he wants to. Before she's up, after she's asleep, or maybe not, since he doesn't want to wake her with his typing. Here and there though, silently on a pad, mornings if she lets him, and she will. She understands and actually likes being by herself to play and read, or he thinks she does. Wishes the marriage had worked out. Wasn't him. And why'd they have a child if it was as bad from the start as she said? Or maybe just was ten to twenty percent him. But of course glad they had her. Ecstatic, everything like that. Nobody could love his kid more, or close to it, even if he isn't such a great father. He can also work the few weeks a year his ex-wife takes her, though if she doesn't, as she didn't last Christmas and won't the end of this summer, he's happy to have her. No, he is; he's not just saying it. Wouldn't care—might even prefer, though it wouldn't be good for Deborah—if his ex-wife didn't spend another sustained period with her.

Look at her. Sun hat off, wiping her brow, maybe to show him how hard she's working, hair stuck over her face by the wind and just sticks there and she has to brush it away, throw it in back. Doesn't recall if that's like her mother and doesn't care to dig back in his memory to find out.

She looks up at him. He waves, she waves, he yells "Working hard?" "Yeah." "Anything growing?" "Lots." "You look so beautiful out there gardening." "How come? I'm sweating. Sweat is ugly, and I'm dirty too." "You just do. I was watching you." "Please don't. I hate when people stare at me. It makes me you-know-what." "Hey, I can do it, I'm your daddy. I was staring because your movements make me happy." "Thank you, even if I don't know what you mean. Boy, the sun's hot." "So come in. What do you want for dinner tonight?" "I can make it." "You kidding—dinner? You already made breakfast and lunch for yourself. We'll go out. The Fish and Pizza, or the Lobster In. Maybe to the lake first for a swim. All I need is to work another hour." "What time is it now?" "Quarter to two." "Work all you want. Till before five. I've lots to do. But can you take me to the library before it closes? I read all the books I got when we came." "We'll do it now. You're more important than my work anytime. Or as much as, each in its own slot." She looks confused. "I'm saying I can do both, have you happy and me happy when I do my work and also happy because you're happy, and so on. Maybe I'll even take the whole day off tomorrow so I can have more time with you." "But you've said you're not happy unless you're working, and that every day if it's not a working day is wasted." "I said that? I must have been lying to myself and through me to you. Anyway, who says I can't change? For you, anything. You don't want to go to camp—you don't, do you?" and she says "No, you know that." "Well, you tried it out, it's not for you this summer, so I shouldn't force you, as you said. But if you later change your mind and want to go, that's okay too, right? Now let's go to the library. Or give me a half-hour at the most."

She knocks on his open door; he jumps. "Sorry if I startled you,

Daddy, but it's been way more than an hour." "My darling, I'm sorry," and opens his arms to her and she steps forward a few feet but not into them. "I got so absorbed in my work. But watch. I'll stop right here, in the middle of a sentence, simply to show you, and prove to myself, I can stop whenever I have to and go back to it when I'm able to and with nothing lost." He covers the typewriter, gets up, they get in the car, are turning onto the main road from the house road when she says "Oh, gosh, I forgot the ones I'm returning." "So we'll go back." "You're not mad?" "Why should I be? It's summer, we got time, plenty of it, and you're my darling. I might even take out a book for pleasure too."

They go back, get her books, after they turn onto the main road again, she says "Tell me about my mother. What was she like when you first met? And I bet you were just as much a nice and smart man then too." "Thanks, but what's to tell? Eventually she said she was bored stiff with me and our marriage and also of our dull university town. I said those weren't sufficient grounds for divorce and that, if she insisted on going, I wanted to keep you. Of course I wanted to keep you anyway, but traditionally, as you know, the mama gets the child. But that's not what you asked. You wanted to know about her. But you know about her. You see her at least two to three weeks a year, plus a few additional days if she happens to be in town or nearby." "That's not nice to her. You're being unfair." "Am I?" "You don't like her anymore?" "I don't mind her. She does what she wants to, and I don't have to be around it anymore. We grew apart. I was sorry we did, for you and me. What else can I tell you, sweetie? I liked to stay put and she liked to get out and away. I had my work, and, other than for having you, she never knew what she wanted to do. I knew this when I married her, even when I first met her, which sort of answers one of your original questions, though maybe that not-stay-putness and no real direction of hers was one of the things—two—that drew me to her. Haven't we spoken of this before?" "Not for a long time. When I was younger you once got very sad and said you once loved her very much and maybe still did." "Was it at night?" "I don't remember." "It probably was, and I was probably drinking too much that night, something I've stopped doing to avoid those kinds of false feelings drinking brings." "That's not at all nice too." "Well, I don't love her anymore, if that's what you're asking.

As to liking her, what's not to like? as my dad used to say about certain things. But I love you, I love grandma, I love my brothers and sort of their kids, and I have good feelings about a few friends, but no love for them or any woman since your mother. And why should I be nice? What's she done for me lately? as my dad also liked to say." "*Daddy.*" "I'm kidding. Or a little. Your mother, she was a beauty. Probably still is. She had a fine mind, maybe still has. Good heart, plenty of energy, adventurous spirit—restless, that's the word I'm looking for and what I think did our marriage in, besides what she finally discovered she didn't see in me. Now she's married to a much more exciting and interesting man. He's in TV; he wears gold beads; he has a physique of someone twenty years younger and likes sports and travel as much as she does. They weekend in Tahiti. He knows everyone, or everyone he has to know. He makes oodles and is loaded with love for her. Let's forget her for now and just enjoy ourselves. Ah, the library. Books, the old bean, simple fish burgers—'Hold the tartar sauce!'—and handfuls of chips. Later a quick sunset dip in salt water at Sandy Point and then ice cream with jimmies. If I only knew someone who had a daughter around your age or there was a girl you met at camp whom you could pal with, that would even be better for you. Not to pawn you off but to enlarge your landscape." "Doesn't matter. It's nice just being with you." "Ah, my dearest, I'd hug you so tight if I wasn't driving."

That night his ex-wife calls, which she does once a week. "How are you?" and she says "Couldn't be better, and you?" "I'll get Deborah." "How is she?" "She'll tell you." "I'm asking you, Harold. Is she having a good time? She said last week she didn't want to go to camp your whole month there. I know you have your own demands, but think it wise to force her to go?" "You're giving me advice from three thousand miles away, or six or eight or ten, however far Tahiti is?" "We're home. And I see nothing wrong in what I said." "Anyway, I took her out of camp Friday, and since then we've been getting along famously, and I hope it'll last the summer and then into the beyond." "Good. That'll be great for you both." "I'll get her." Puts the receiver down, picks it up. "And oh, she asked about you today. No strange coincidence, since I'm sure you're on her mind a lot, particularly since she won't be visiting you this summer, and she probably knew you were calling tonight,

BATTERED HEAD

81

Monday, your call night." "I could call other days and more often. I guess the week goes so fast, and I got into a routine." "Anyway, she asked what I thought of you. Then, not so much now. I told her of now and some of then. My feelings, et cetera—" "What did you say about your feelings?" "Oh, you know, that I loved you then but not now and wondered why in hell you ever married me. That I'd even warned you about what it'd come to." "Why'd you tell her that? It was unnecessary. She's too young. You went too far." "Well, I didn't exactly say it; I intimated. Also intimated I was glad you thought it better I should have her than you. No, I didn't say that either or intimate. But it's what I thought. Glad your restlessness made you a world traveler and first-class self-seeker and not a stay-at-homenik, since that way I got her. That's all." "Why'd you bring all that up to me? I've no bad feelings to you. There's a reason I couldn't have her here this summer. I'm pregnant and I have to stay in bed most of the time and right up to the delivery, since, if you must know, I've already had two miscarriages with Tim. But this one's coming along fine. I've passed the critical period but still have to be careful. And I called specifically tonight—I was going to let her tell you this if she wanted—to tell her I'm pregnant and that she's going to have a very kid sister. We only got all the clinical results last Friday. I was also planning to tell her I'm going to be a much different mother this time around, as well as a vastly changed one to her, and that if she wants, once I have the baby, she can spend whole summers with us. Next one, for instance, and maybe whole years." "If she wants? Oh no, you're going to ruin it for me," and hangs up. She calls back. "Will you let me speak to her?" "She's asleep." "Who's asleep?" his daughter says from the next room. "Please put her on." Puts her on, watches her as she talks. She's thrilled, says "That's fantastic, Mom; it's great. I'm so happy I can practically cry." At what, sister or idea of living with her mother? When she gets off, she says "Know what Mommy told me?" "Whatever it is, you can't. I let you get out of camp, but I'm not going to let you get out of everything." "What are you talking about?" "What did your mommy say?" "She's having a baby—a girl. I'll have a little sister, and I can help name her. She and Tim want me to. She says they're stuck for good names that aren't too popular." "Oh, you're so lucky. I only had two brothers and from the same parents. They were older and end up beating you up before they get real nice to you. But they were closer in age to me than you two will be, and you'll be much older, so she can't beat you up. You'll be a terrific older sister. I wish I had you as one." "Then you couldn't have me as a daughter." "Hey, that's true, I didn't think of that. Too bad."

She asks him to tell her a story that night. He does every night, or a continuation of one. Tonight he puts the chapter story on hold, he says, and starts a new one called "Two Sisters." "Sadie and Sally," he says. "Awful names," she says. "Not ones I'd give." "They're like twins, though they don't dress alike and are several years apart, maybe even nine. Once Sadie was born they started doing almost everything together, or when she started to walk and talk." He gives examples. "Then a war came. Their parents had to fight in the army, so Sadie went with an uncle and Sally with an aunt." He's silent. "What happens next?" she says. "I don't know. I'm trying to figure it out. The war goes on for five years. Their parents have disappeared. Nobody knows if they were killed in battle or taken prisoner and not returned or got lost somewhere and are in another terrible country trying to get out, or what." "This is too sad to listen to before I go to sleep, even if everyone finds one another." "They don't find each other so fast. The separation goes on longer than the war. The uncle and aunt die of natural causes—heart disease, old age; they're actually a great-uncle and great-aunt. The sisters live completely separate lives for more than ten years after the war. Their parents are dead." "Oh Daddy, I'll have nightmares now." "I'm sorry. Erase the story." "You can't. I already heard it." "Then I'll change it." "How? It already happened. The sisters could meet again but their parents are dead." "I can change it if I want. I made a mistake. I got the wrong lives into my characters." "You know you didn't. Why'd you tell it if you knew it was going to be so scary and sad? Do you want me to have bad dreams?" "Of course not. I just didn't know what I was telling you. Maybe I'm still suffering a little from some after-bang effects from that accident last week on my head. Or we were talking about you and your future sister, I started telling a story about two other sisters, and then I got carried away or didn't know I was telling it." "You had to know. You always do when you tell me a story." "Sometimes things get in from somewhere deep in you that you're not aware of. The unconscious, the subconscious—you know, we've talked of it. So maybe I did it, though I didn't realize or intend it, because I want you to live with me till you go to college, and even in college if you want to go to the one I teach at or another one in the area. And I thought, or those deeper things in me I wasn't aware of thought, that the story would make you stay with me more. Because I fear your mother will take you from me. Rather, that you'll want to live with her more. That even if you're legally mine—meaning, that I've legal custody of you till you're of the age of consent . . . Is that it, age of consent? Till you're of legal age to say where you want to live—even alone, if you want—and I couldn't do anything about it, then I could . . . I could what? I lost my train of thought. You remember what I started out saying?" "No." "I guess it was that your mother will make life very attractive for you living with her and Tim and the baby. Occasionally in Tahiti and mostly in California and all their trips abroad and with an attitude that'll probably be more liberal than mine. And that you'll want to live with them permanently, and I won't be able to deny you because I'll want you to be happy so long as it's safe there and so on, which I'm sure it'll be. And then I'll only see you a few days during the regular year if they happen to fly to the East Coast and also a month in the summer, even two if you want, but not enough for me. And maybe you'll say you're so happy there, or they're doing such great things summers, that you won't want to come East to me, and then what would I do? Maybe I should get married again just to have another child in case you leave. Would you stay with me over your mother if I had another child, even if it was a boy?" "You can't have a child." "The woman I married, I mean, but you knew that. Anyway, it's way off the point. I'll tell you what I told your mother when she first said she was leaving me—maybe I shouldn't say this to you." "Don't, Daddy, if you don't think you should." "No, it's okay, it's not bad, and I know what I'm saying here, it's not coming from somewhere else. You ought to go if you feel you have to, that's all I said. Oh damn," because she looks sad, "by your face I can tell I shouldn't have said it. Blame my poor head. Or just blame me. But don't cry, okay? Just don't cry." "I won't. I'm not feeling like it. But it's nice she wants me to live with her after so long, isn't it?" "Yes it is. Or at least if you think so. That's the attitude I should take. That's the one I will. Because it is good she wants you. It's never too late to change, and you've got all those young years left. And now I'm looking for something to end this conversation with, all right, sweetheart?" "Good night, Daddy. I'm tired. See you in the morning." "First kiss me good night and brush your teeth and go to bed. But you already brushed your teeth and are in bed. Good night, sweetheart," and kisses her and leaves the room.

Later he thinks of his ex-wife. That scumbag, that wretch, she *would*, and goes into his daughter's room, sits on the floor and leans his head on her bed and says "My darling, my dearest, I know you can't hear me, I don't know why I'm even talking like this, but please don't leave me, not at least till you're of age." "Daddy, what's wrong?" and he says "Oh, nothing, go back to sleep, dear. I only came in to see that you're covered," and pats her forehead and leaves.

He drinks a little, reads, takes off his clothes and starts exercising vigorously for the first time since he cut his head. The light's on; he does the same ones he did that night. "So that's why I didn't see the chair I hit," he says. "I close my eyes when I exercise."

TURNING
THE
CORNER

He calls every place he can think of and not one of them has it. He goes downtown and complains. "You don't have it. How come, what's wrong, why you holding it up?" They say "What are you talking about?" He says "You say you don't know? Maybe you really don't know, maybe that's why it's being held up. If that's the case, case closed. I mean, if that's the case, well, case closed. Meaning, well, if that's the situation, that you haven't got it because you don't know what I'm talking about, then I shouldn't bother about it anymore, wouldn't you say, or is that overstating the case?"

They slam the door on him. First they edge him out of the store. Then past the door into the street. Then they slam the door on him, lock it. He knows they locked it because he tries opening the door and the knob won't turn all the way. The door's made of glass, and he knocks on it. Raps, really, raps. The man and woman behind the door pull the shade down so he can't see through the glass. Or for another reason, or a slew of them, like the shade down is a sign to him to go away, or so that they can't see him. But a shade, he thinks. Very old-fashioned. He remembers shades like this when he was a boy. Candy stores had them. Closed for the day, down went the shade. You didn't have to have a Closed sign on the door, for the shade down meant the store was closed for the day or just temporarily; for instance, if the owner went out for lunch. No, then the owner, or manager, or just the only person working there would usually put an Out to Lunch sign on the door or Be Back At 1:30 or something, or even a cardboard clock on the door with the hands pointed to 1:30 and Be Back At above the clock on the same sign. He knocks some more, raps, but by now has already given up. Rapped for effect. He'd have been surprised, very, if one of them had opened the door or even let the shade up.

He doesn't know what to do now. He wants to get it but so far no one has it, and he doesn't know if they even know what exactly it is he wants and, if they did know, whether they could ever get it. Maybe it isn't around anymore, doesn't exist anywhere. But he wants it very badly, that's for sure. Maybe a completely different kind of store will have it or know where he can get it. He sees many different kinds of stores but selects one that's completely different from the last one he tried. That one he found by just getting out of the subway station and going into the first store he saw. On the phone, same thing. He opened the phone directory's business pages and chose at random a few stores to call. One was a bakery, another a dry cleaner's, another a sporting goods store. Now he tries a walk-in dental office.

The receptionist, at least the person behind a counter right past the door, says "Can I help you?" He tells her what he wants. She says "You've come to the right place, all right. Please fill this out," and hands him a questionnaire and pen. He says "I have? I must? Well, this has got to be my lucky day, I think." He sits and starts filling out the questionnaire. What's his name? He forgets. What's his address? Doesn't know if he has one. What city does he live in, what state, what's his zip code, phone number, profession, age? He doesn't know, he's not quite sure, he's trying to think what city this is, what state. But concentrate on the city. If it comes, maybe the rest of the information will, like the shade. Meaning: workday starts, up goes the shade, and there's light. Something like that. So: Is this the city he was born in, grew up in, went to grade school in, college in, worked a number of years in, married in, had children in, now lives in? Was he ever married, did he ever have children, does he have a phone number? If he does, what could it be? He's had lots of phone numbers. Good, that's a start. 662-3218. 529-5396. 764-3152. 462-4830. He can remember about a dozen. But he doesn't know what previous or present residence of his corresponds to what number, what city with what number, even what part of his life with what number. But those are some of the numbers he's had. He could give more. 448-2623. 724-4706. 816-0029. Maybe he should call several of those and find out where he's lived. Maybe even one of those numbers will be the number where he now lives, if he does live anyplace. Some were work numbers, he thinks, so he also might find out what he did and where. But he doesn't remember the area code of any of them, or at least the right area code for even one of them. So all the numbers, if he reaches any, would be in this city, and the name of the city is still a blank. More questions: Social Security number, wife's name, children's names, is he married, divorced, single, or is his spouse deceased? He can't answer any of the questions, except what sex he is and his Social Security number—099-63-5124—though he's not sure if that's his wife's number, if he has or had one, one of his children's, if he had any, or even for some reason his mother's or father's, or is he just making the number up? Worst of all, he thinks, is he still can't remember his name. As a kid he does remember he had a cat named Pat. "Pat Pat," his mother used to say and he'd pat Pat. "Pet Rex," his father used to say and he'd pet Rex, but who and what was Rex?—he thinks the next-door dog. "Pet and pat this," his wife or some other woman or girl used to say, and he'd pet and pat that, but what? He thinks now he had two wives and that they had the same first name, but one had an "e" at the end of it and the other didn't.

He goes up to the receptionist, if that's what she is, and says "It seems I won't be able to get what I want here because I can't answer any of the questions on the questionnaire except my sex and possibly my Social Security number. Not even, if you can believe it, my name, first or last; I don't know if I had a middle one or middle initial. But suddenly everything's a blank. Not suddenly; just now. I think I knew what the answers to most or all of these questions were before I got here. But now, I hold the pencil in my hand— excuse me; ball-point pen—and put it over the lines I'm supposed to write things in, like my name and address, and nothing comes out, and not because there's no ink in it. There should be plenty unless this is a defective pen, but it looks brand new. Just suddenly, well, I'm repeating myself, but anyway, just suddenly I don't remember any names, ages, relations, addresses, nothing but that Social Security number and almost a score of phone numbers without their area codes, if I'm sure what a score is. I doubt any of that will be of much use unless you want to try a lot of those phone numbers alone or with various area codes, and why would you? As for the Social Security number, I'm not even sure it's mine. Is there a way to check? It might be a start."

"There could be," she says, and he gives her the number, she calls an office, after a long wait the office gives her a name, she says "Is your name this?" and shows him it and he says "I think so, it looks familiar," and she says "Then we do have a start," and looks up the name in the phone book, and there's only one listing of it, and she shows him the address and says "Is that where you live?" and he says "It could be, for it's also familiar," and she says "And the phone number, is it yours?" and he says "I'm not sure; it does seem familiar. But so do some of the numbers below it, but none of their names and addresses," and he starts saying all the phone numbers he knows and one of them is that phone number, and none is one of the numbers below it, and she says "Then it must be you, or there's as good a chance it is as there isn't, if not a little better, though I really don't know the odds in all that, I'm just guessing—want me to call it?" and he says "Please do, but if I'm the only one living there, and there isn't a cleaning lady cleaning it there right now, let's say, then nobody will answer, for I'm here," and she says "Probably, but let's see."

She dials. "Yes, hello," a man says loudly, and she says "Hello, I'm looking for Roland Hirsch," and he says "Speaking," and she says "You're Roland Hirsch?" and he says "I am indeed, what can I do for you? Though I want to remind you, young lady, and you are a young lady, am I correct?" and she says "I still consider myself young, whatever that has to do with it, as do my husband and children—consider me young—but anyway, Mr. Hirsch," and he says "Well anyway to you, young lady, for my warning is that if this is a solicitation of any kind, and by that I mean for a business or charity or for anything like that, then I don't wish to continue speaking, since I don't use my phone for any other purpose but personal phone calls," and she says "That's good—that's really very good, in fact, and what I should be saying to all the callers who canvass and solicit me on my home phone. But what if this was a dental office calling to remind you of your 3:30 appointment with Dr. Lembro tomorrow—would you consider that a business or personal phone call?" and he says "Do I have an appointment?" and she says "I believe you do, Mr. Hirsch, it was made for you six months ago—just a checkup and cleaning," and he says "Well thanks for reminding me, and yes, I'd consider it not only a personal phone call but a very useful one indeed. So I'll see you tomorrow, if you'll be there," and she says "It's my day off, tomorrow, but someone just as accommodating will be here to see to your needs," and hangs up.

"Wait a minute," he says. "How is it that the man who has an appointment here tomorrow has the same name as the person who I think is me?" and she says "I told you you came to the right place," and he says "That's what you consider an answer? For I'm saying, how can that man be Roland Hirsch if I'm supposed to be him, and there was only one Roland Hirsch in the phone book?" and she says "The answers to that can be considerable, some of which you even hinted at before yourself. For instance, you aren't Roland Hirsch. Or you are, but you live in another city, and the incident just now with this Roland Hirsch was only a coincidence. Or you are, again, Roland Hirsch, and you do live in this city, but your phone's unlisted, and you only know this Roland Hirsch's number because of one to a number of reasons, maybe some of them unfathomable but others not. For instance, you might know it because out of curiosity one day you looked up your name in this city's phone book and saw someone else had it. That's a legitimate possibility, and even one if you didn't live in this city—you might have only been visiting and looked up your name in the phone book and found it. Or you could live in this city, or even not, and be unlisted here though not necessarily unlisted if you live in another city, but be Roland Hirsch, Jr., and he's Sr., and you're somehow related, son and father, cousin and cousin, nephew and uncle, because his senior could be to a different junior. Or for all we know, he could even be a junior, but he chose to give up that part of his name once his father died, which is why it's not in the phone book that way, or because he didn't like being called junior.

Or maybe you're not junior either and he's not senior and was never a junior, and you're completely unrelated, and you're both just plain Roland Hirsch, he with his middle initial, you with yours or even, by some coincidence, the same as his, if Roland Hirsch is your name. But taking one thing at a time, since Roland Hirsch isn't the most common name, are you a junior and is your father alive and was that his phone number and address and does he still have teeth that need fixing or just a cleaning and checkup?"

"Yes," he says, "he does have teeth, or did the last time I remember seeing him—all of them, and he is a senior, though why it's not in the phone book that way I don't know; maybe it's a phone company mistake. Anyway, that's what I was looking for all along—not a thing but a he, a man, my dad, husband of my mother, who's also alive and what I've been looking for, though she's lost just about all her teeth and mostly wore plates. Did he mention anything about her? No, I know he didn't, at least in that last call, for I heard every word he said. But great, I came to the right place, all right, though how you knew I don't know, for I was never specific to you about what I wanted," and she says "Oh, I knew when you came in so unspecifically that it was something we could do for you. For you see, people deal with their fears of dentists in all kinds of ways, and one of them is through complete amnesia: 'Who are you? What am I doing here?'—that sort of thing. Or to say something like, when they first see me as they come in, 'I'll have a frank with plenty of mustard and sauerkraut'— anything to deceive themselves they're not here to have their teeth fixed or extracted or even cleaned, for even that can hurt. Let's face it, we all, so to speak, meet our maker or destroyer in different ways, though some of us, like me, prefer to meet him or her straight on."

"Well thank you, thank you," he says, "and I don't think I'll be needing this now," giving her back the questionnaire and clipboard it's on, and she says "The pen," and he says "Right," and takes it out of his pocket—"You can't believe how many pencils and pens I've accumulated this way"—and she says "Not from this office, you don't," and he says "Right, I can see that," and leaves, takes the bus downtown, walks across the bridge, walks another two miles to get to the address he saw by his father's name in the phone book.

"Yes?" his father says on the intercom, and he says "It's me,

Junior," and his father says "God, you've been gone a long time. Do you really think it's worth it for me to come down to see what you look like?" and he says "How's Mom?" and his father says "Your mother? My dear boy, she's been gone a long long time." "Gone where?" and his father says "Gone to rest, my son, to rest," and he says "Not dead," and his father says "Dead, my dear son, dead." "Dad, please come down and help me, I don't think I'm ready to face this yet. I'm not. I'll never be," and his father says "Nobody is, my dear son, nobody, and neither was I, but I was only her lover and husband and closest friend and father of her children and then of her only surviving child, not her flesh and blood. I'll be right down."

He waits there. Day becomes night; warmth, cold. He's not dressed for it, he thinks, and rings the bell. Nobody answers. Rings and rings and nobody answers. If this were an apartment house, he thinks, he'd ring several bells to get in. But it's a private home, and he just sits on the steps, hoping his father will come down.

A police car stops in the street, the policewoman says through the car window "Is there a good reason you're sitting there, sir?" and he says "No, officer, there isn't, and I'll be on my way," and gets up and goes. When he's at the corner he looks back, thinking if the officer's gone he'll go back and ring some more and maybe even make a commotion under the windows, but she's sitting in the car, now peeling and eating what looks to be an orange or tangerine. Then she looks his way, points her stick out the window at him, and he turns the corner.

LOST

He's called at his office. Something unspeakable's happened. "What is it?" Come home quick, the caller says, his wife needs him. "Why, what's wrong, something with her?" His daughter. "What, what is it?" Come home now. "Just tell me, then I'll be right home. Is she hurt? Was she hit by a car? Is she dead?" She was on her way home from school—"A car? Is she alive?" She's dead. A fight started between several boys and girls a block from school. Some-one pulled out a gun—a kid, they don't know if it was a boy or girl. They don't even think this kid was one of the ones fighting. Every-thing happened so fast. Some shots were fired. One went into her head.

After it's all over—the medical inquest, funeral, reporters at his door—weeks later, he tries to go back to work. Before then, he couldn't leave the apartment. He and his wife stayed in their bed-room most of the time, sleeping, staring, talking very little. People came every day—friends, relatives—shopped and cooked for them, cleaned the place, answered the phone. Then his wife said one morning "I guess it's time to face life; what do you think?" He said "You face it, I'm not going anywhere yet; who knows when I'll be ready." She started cooking, shopping, continued with her translating work, even returned some overdue books to the library and paid the fines, checked out a few, resumed reading, though still didn't want to look at a newspaper. He stayed in the bedroom. A week later he came out, ran around the block once, and a few days later headed for work.

It's awful for him on the street going to the subway. There are little girls his daughter's age going to school in groups or with a parent or nanny. Awful on the subway. Girls, boys, a few years older than his daughter, some reading, studying, others playful, a few looking like killers, or ones who want to be. She loved to read, was a terrific student, liked being playful with him, as he did with her. He got off after a few stops and cabbed home. Stayed in the apartment a few more days, helped his wife with things like cooking and cleaning, read her translations for corrections. Then he went back to work.

People there: "We're sorry," "I'm sorry," "We're all tremendously sorry, words can't express it." He says "Please, I don't want to hear of it, I don't want to discuss it, and I especially don't want any sympathies or condolences or regrets or things like that. I just want to forget, I just want to forget, I just want to forget, so please don't." But every so often someone says something that makes him burst out crying in front of the person or run into one of the bathroom stalls to do it. "My kid's suddenly doing lousy at school, and we don't know what to do about it. Oops, forgive me." "I gotta be home early tonight—it's my girl's birthday, and all this when I've a ton of work here to do, but my wife says I have to. Oh, jeez, I forgot, excuse me."

"I can't face the world, I can't live with myself, I can't forget her, I don't know what to do, I want her back, I want her here now, I can't sleep nights, I walk around in a daze most of the day, I don't think I'll ever be able to lie in bed or be out of it with my mind on anything but her, I can't live in this apartment, I see her room, I see the dinner table, the silverware, sink she dumped the dishes in, goddamn pot she shit in, streets she ran and skated on up and down, kids she played with or who look like the ones she did, elevator she rode up on, doormen she spoke to, shop windows she looked at, reflection of herself she caught or caught me catching her admiring herself, you name it, it's there, the works." All this to his wife. She says "Don't you think I feel the same? But what am I supposed to do, get sick and crack up or die over it and not be there for you?" "Of course, I'm sorry," he says, "I know you think of her as much if not more than I. Certainly at least as much. But it's become so individual though. For all the reasons that it would."

They move to an apartment across town—he insists. Costs them twice the rent and for less space, but the hell with it, he couldn't live where they were. "It's the only way," he told his wife, "plus giving away just about everything she owned or used, that I think I can make it, or for the next couple of years or so." He sees girls her age in the new neighborhood. He expected to but hoped his reaction wouldn't be the same. One girl he thinks looks almost exactly like her. If he saw her from maybe ten feet away but didn't know his daughter was dead, he'd at first think it was her. The long light hair well-brushed, same solid build, tall height, style of clothes, bulging forehead, high cheeks, eyeglasses with big eyes, skin, neck, little nose. He follows her awhile, imagines he's following his daughter for fun though isn't so out of it that he really thinks he is, then says to himself "This is nuts," and turns back.

He can't pass schools once he knows where they are on his routes. Can't even stand hearing kids shouting from classroom windows. Almost every time he sees girls her age laughing, he starts to cry, or stops whatever he's doing—walking, reading— and closes his eyes to give himself time to get over being choked up. He doesn't know what to do. "Maybe I can get a job somewhere else. You could do your translating anywhere—out in the country, let's say, and maybe even in a different country where I don't understand the language. Though kids' laughing and giggling and stuff would be the same anywhere, I think, and I probably couldn't get the same kind of work anywhere but in a city and in this country. But I could commute to the city. And we of course should start making love again and have another child if it's not too late." "We can try," she says.

They try, and she can't conceive. It may be something missing in him or her. They take tests to find out what might be wrong, and nothing shows up. "Maybe it's my disposition," he says, "or ours. I've never heard where that has anything to do with it, but it does affect some illnesses, doctors have said, maybe even cause them, so it could with this." He's always sad, or close to it. One night while they're in bed he says "You know, I don't think I've smiled once since Lynn died. Oh my God," and he cries, and when he comes out of it he says "That was the first time I've said her name, or even said the word 'died' when I was alluding to her, since that thing happened. That thing, that thing," and cries some more. "I cry as much as you," she says. "I don't mean for this to be competitive grieving or anything, but I want you to know I still think of her almost all the time and get very little sleep because of her, like you," and he says "I assumed that; I really did," and kisses her and turns off the light on his side.

A few months later he says "Maybe I should begin facing it, talk to people about it, even bring it up out of the blue sometimes. Not to a professional but just people who have wanted to express their sympathies to me for months but I've fought them off. Yeah, I'll try that. I think I can swing it." She says "If you think it's a good idea, do it. But I still feel you should see a therapist, even mine if you want. He's wonderful—smart, sharp, caring—and he already knows from me how you feel and what Lynn's murder has done to you. And maybe he would even see us together about it, at other times, which is also what I've been wanting. And you remember, I was never a great believer in it before this, but he's certainly helped me." He says "Nah, what's good for you might not be for me. For now, just regular people."

At work he says to his closest colleague "Sven, if you want I'm ready to talk about my daughter now. You know, Lynn. There. You can't believe how tough it is to even say her name aloud; even in my head, if there's a reason for it. But there, I've said it and I'm not falling down, am I? What I'm actually saying is I have to talk about her, have to, do you mind?" Sven says "You know how I felt about it and still do—heartbroken—and you can come to me anytime. But probably the best guy to talk about this to is Boris Lehman in Sales. He lost a son a few years back when some crazy kids started shooting up a subway car. His son was going to school, though, not coming back." And he says "Maybe he would be a good person to speak with."

He calls Boris, and they meet for lunch. "How'd you get over it," he says, "or at least where you could begin functioning like a seminormal human being?" and Boris says "For a while I didn't think I ever would. But I came out of it a little when I found out there were at least three other people in this organization who'd lost their kids this way, or maybe one lost his wife, who got it in the grade school she taught at. But anyway, to these deranged spontaneous shootouts or just individual slaughters. One was the guy who still cleans my office—Hudson. His kid was out roller-skating and got caught in the cross fire when two teenage drug dealers started popping off at each other with automatics. Fortunately for Hudson, he had three kids and a wife who was pregnant, not that it still didn't nearly kill him at the time, he said. Like you, I only had my one, and that little fellow took eight steady years of mating to get. And then Clarence Fangel in Publicity downstairs, ten years ago his daughter was stabbed to death. Something about some other girl in her high school who thought she was trying to steal her boyfriend away . . . "

He speaks to Hudson and Fangel and learns there are a few more people in the building and the ones around it who lost their kids or younger siblings this way: shot, stabbed, pushed in front of a train, thrown off a roof after being gang-raped. There's even a lunchtime support group in this business district for such people, and he goes to a few meetings, but the stories he hears, instead of helping him, make him feel even worse. "You got to give it time," the group leader tells him, when he says he's thinking of leaving it, and he says "I'm sure what everyone here's going through is as inconsolable to them as I am to what's going on in me, but something chemical or whatever must be in me where the feeling can't be reversed. But I'll give it its due." Finally at one meeting some new woman, a copywriter in his building, tells the group of her two-year-old twins a few months ago when she was making a phone call on the street from a public booth, and he rushes out with his hands over his ears, goes home, pulls down the shades in his bedroom and later, when his wife comes home, tells her he doesn't know if he'll ever leave. "Forget the country. Forget another country. From what I heard in the group it's not a lot better anyplace else, and there's more and more of it every day. Also forget about having another child, with or without my sperm, or even one we adopt. The times just aren't right for bringing kids up."

He quits his job. His wife tells him he has to do something else besides stay in his room, "For this way you'll get even worse than crazy. Maybe you can work in some way against the kind of violence that killed Lynn. Get a job teaching kids in school, or after school, or with an organization that fights such violence, or just work at your old job to have enough money to give to places and schools that fight or just study such violence." He says "Best I can do is just to be talked about as someone whose grieving for his daughter totally disabled him for anything but staying in his room. Maybe that piece of information will filter down to people who are violent and prone to killing other young people . . . Nah, who am I my kidding? I had a daughter, loved my daughter, lost her and now grieve every waking second for her. Maybe one day I'll come out of it, but right now I don't think I will."

They still sleep together, but he finds it very difficult to make love anymore. She says "I want a child desperately. It's the only way I'll become relatively sane again myself. I love you and don't want to lose you, but would you consent to a divorce so I can possibly meet someone else and try to have a child or adopt a child as a single parent?" "I think that's fair," he says. "I know I could never have another kid. I'd be so protective I'd squeeze the life out of it, send it to a shrink by the time it was five and maybe, because of my terrible parenting, turn it into a violent kid who hurts other children and maybe even kills them."

They divorce, he moves out of the apartment so she can have it, moves in with his sister in another part of the country. She looks after him, gets him his food, cleans his room and clothes, doesn't complain. "Who do I have but you?" she says, since her husband divorced her soon after they lost their only child to disease. "Oh my God, I forgot that," he says. "It must be just as bad for you as it is for me. What am I saying? It is; I know; I should have been taking care of you then in some way, but I didn't." "You gave me lots of sympathy, and I was married at the time, so that was enough. Now, what is it?—ten years later—I can take care of myself just fine."

Eventually he gets out—it takes a couple of years—gets a job as a salesman in a department store, still thinks of Lynn a number of times every day, and sometimes so much he has to quit work for the day and go home, drinks too much lots of nights to blot her out of his head, pays half the rent and upkeep of his sister's place, learns that his wife remarried and adopted two children, sends her kids gifts every year for their birthdays and Christmas, never goes out with women, makes no friends, every now and then does have lunch in the employee cafeteria with a few of the same co-workers, goes through life like this, feels lucky he can get through every day without cracking up and that he's able to make even a marginal living. His sister does well at work, has many interests, several boyfriends, sometimes stays out all night with them, goes to parties, takes vacations, knows lots of women she calls buddies. He tells her "That's the way it ought to be, I guess."

THE
VICTOR

Way it happened. The chairperson of the committee is called up to the stage podium by the head of the American Fiction Foundation. Rob is sitting at one of the many tables, holding his wife's hand. He leans closer to her and says in her ear "I know I'm not going to win." "Wait and see," she whispers; "you never know. Though you're not expecting it, are you?" "Nah, I know who they're going to give it to; at least not to me. Because when it comes down to it at the end, the establishment, right? Onwards and always. But why'd you say 'you never know'?" "Shh, she's talking." A couple of people at the table—his editor and publisher—are smiling at him; then the editor starts grinning. He smiles back and looks at the opened program on his lap. They know something? They smile because they know he's won but were told not to say anything, or because he's lost and they don't want to reveal it with a serious expression. But why her almost ecstatic grin? Maybe she has a problem faking a smile around so many people, or she's the only one at the table who knows he's won and she can't keep her exhilaration in. He looks around at several other tables. A few people are looking at him, but no smiles, nothing serious, just with interest, as if "How does a person appear at such a time in his life? And if he wins, I want to see his immediate reaction, since he is the one sitting closest and facing me, and if he loses, well that too."

The chairperson's going on about the "distinguished history of this prestigious award," mentions several recent winners and the book titles, "all of which, I'm told, are still in print, no doubt because of their high quality but I'm sure also because of the recognition the prize gives," the healthy state of American fiction today, based on her judging experience the past half-year, "so if anyone tells you of the present or possible demise of written fiction in this country, you send him or her to me," and finally "the long arduous job of the five judges, all working fiction writers themselves, in choosing this year's winner. We each read the more than three hundred entries in book form or galleys. Or, to be vulnerably honest, only segments of some of them—after all, we're only humans and writers with just so much human and writing time—to come up with the five finalists, and met today in this hotel to make our decision: Lemuel Pond. The winner of the American Fiction Award is Lemuel Pond for his novel *Eyeball*, published by Sklosby Press, edited by—"

Lights go to Pond's table; he slaps his head with both hands as if he can't believe it. Rob looks at his wife—she's already looking sympathetically at him and squeezes his hand—then at the editor and publisher. They're smiling at him, or trying to, the publisher sticking up his fist and jiggling it, whatever that's supposed to mean; the editor now wiping her eyes with a table napkin. "Fuck them," Rob mouths to his wife. She puts her finger over her lips. Pond gets up, most people in the ballroom are applauding, a few whistling and shouting, and starts walking around the tables to the stage, people patting him and grabbing his hand, and one man kissing it as he goes. "That jerk didn't deserve it," Rob says to his wife over the noise, "that's all I'll say. It's a piece of shit, what he wrote, so of course you have to expect they'll reward it, the gutless judges, the toadying foundation, the scummy big stiffs of the publishing world here, our little guys excluded." She puts her mouth to his ear. "Don't say any more, really; someone will hear. And especially not to any reporters if they ask, or anyone tonight. Give it a day. I'm sorry, darling. You should have got it, and it's what you're saying, but it's over, so go along with it or you'll regret it." "Not so much me," he says, moving his head away, "but really almost any one of the other three. But he's an amateur. Albeit, a first-class one, which accounts, doesn't it? for all the newspapers and highfalutin magazines that slavered over it in reviews, the biggest hype job of them all by a writer from the same smelly Sklosby stable. 'Oh! Can't he much! Can't he perfectly! One of our precious traditional own. Oh! Oh!' " "Enough. Really, enough. People have to be looking, and they eat up this stuff."

"Okay." He reaches for his wine glass; it's empty. "Fancy dinner, right? With white for the ap and red for the main, and the waiters refilling your glass second you set it down. But when you truly need a drink, they're not around. Maybe it's the first sign of being the loser." He grabs her glass, which is full. "Mind?" "No, drink away, though don't get loaded. This thing's not going to do that to you, is it? We have to drive back tomorrow." "And if I'd won?" "Then you'd be entitled, I guess, to fall on your face or to at least get high. But I'd probably still ask you to be moderate, if only to get us a cab back to the hotel, and they'd probably want you to hang around tomorrow for interviews."

"Listen," he says, drinking, "I'm not disappointed, no matter what I might sound like. Because how could I be, for I told you days ago, didn't I?—weeks. Pond, first and fabmost, with his high-powered backing and their thousand and one contacts, not to mention his handsome renegotiated advance. If they'd given the award to me and my little publisher and unhotshot editor and no agent or to speak of advance, half this joint would be empty next year. For the biggies pay for the event and the foundation and want returns for their own and on what they put in and certainly no threatening precedents, so they wouldn't take it nicely if the nobody from nowhere won. But the victor's speechmaking, so we gotta show our proper respects," and he turns, smiles at his still smiling-tearful editor, who's maybe still tearful because she sees how disappointed he is. He waves to her. "Don't worry, I'm in great shape," raises his shoulders and gestures with his hands and face "So what else did we expect?" and she nods and they both face the stage.

Pond is finished saying what eloquent writers all the finalists are and the stiff competition their books gave to the point where he never thought he had a chance to win, and is now saying he's going to use the platform this award gives by "helping to combat illiteracy in Latin America, where, as some of you may know, most of my novel, other than for its brief flashbacks, takes place. I will also, in any way I'm able to, like lecturing in schools and libraries, use the same platform to promote serious reading in this country of not only fiction but poetry, philosophy, history, the sciences—" "Biography," someone shouts out and people laugh, and Pond, laughing, says "Biography, autobiography, whichever this gentleman writes, edits or even publishes . . . belles-lettres," he reads, "essays, well, the whole kit and caboodle, I'll call it, of fine writing." Then he thanks his editor, agent, publisher, the marketing people at Sklosby, "for it isn't easy these days selling, though I'm sure this award will help—indeed, I know—what is fundamentally a nonmarketable literary novel. And they did a wow of a job and have my profound thanks and respect, as does anyone in any capacity in publishing who was involved with my book. And last," to his wife, who several times forced him to forge on with the novel in progress when he'd only wanted to toss it into the garbage, and he asks that the spotlight be directed to their table, where she stands, waves, blows a kiss to him, he blows one back, audience applauds, he says "See ya in a second, honey," thanks the judges and foundation again, waves the statuette he received and in the other hand the envelope with the ten thousand dollar check. Then he leaves the stage, side-jacket-pockets the envelope as he goes to his table, is swamped by people there, autographs books, has his back slapped, cheeks kissed, is whispered to by people seated on both sides of him and standing behind, poses for photos, is escorted by foundation officials to some Louis the Someteenth room for a press conference, and as he's leaving the ballroom waiters rush in with the main course.

"God, I forgot, got to make a phone call," Rob says, and his wife says "To whom and about what?" and he says "My sweetheart. To tell her I don't have the dough or ennoblement now to run away with her. Ned at the *Globe*, though at his home. He's been so nice about it all. Publicizing my finalism and sudden leap to quick descent, and also getting the book a long review there, and he said to call, win or lose, but collect. The kids, your folks, my mom, I guess

I can now forget," and kisses her lips, goes out the side entrance near their table, sees Pond leaving the men's room and hurrying with some people through the corridor outside. "Pond," he yells, and waves, and Pond waves and says "I wish it had been you." A reporter, badge and no tux, takes this down. "Thanks, same here. I mean, it was you, so congratulations, nice job," but Pond, smiling and raising his hands helplessly as if he'd like to shout in the corridor some more, is ushered into a room with the group, and door's closed. "I bet he hasn't read a page of my book," he says to himself low. "Or maybe a page or two and thought 'Doesn't look bad, but I probably opened it up on the best parts,' and put it back on the rack. Lucky fuck. Hey reporter, take that down."

Calls Ned and says "Hi, it's Rob, and look it, I didn't want to call collect but you said to," and Ned says "No hassle, buddy, glad you could make it. So, match is over, what's the score?" and he says "Pond, probably five to nothing, so title it 'Zero Wins.' I'm sorry, I shouldn't have said that. Sounds sour." "Pond, huh? I'm surprised. The money was on Buckley," and he says "Really, Buckley? I thought it was between Pond and Kendler, with a distant long shot, me. Who said Buckley? I mean, though she's another, like Kendler and Pond, from a major house and no doubt with a hot young agent and fancy editor and connections, her book barely got quotable reviews," and Ned says "That was just the *Times*. But we loved it, as did all the prepubs, and other reviewers I spoke to and people in publishing and some writers who thought they knew. Almost a sure thing, seemed like, and maybe even a Pulitzer as well." "You never told me that," and Ned says "Come on, I didn't want to ruin your New York party with speculation, and look what it produced. But you felt you had a chance?" and he says "Me? Small-time Schlermy with his tricky monster of a tome? Hey, you lift it in one hand and say 'Uncarryable, therefore unreadable, at least not reviewable,' except for you, and pick up lighter and cheaper bulk. Only, I thought, if the judges were high on something or feeling very rebellious and pugnacious or maybe just good-natured but willing to buck the power people and take the afterbrunt. You know, because mine was less traditional, we'll say, and possibly even more adventurous in the way I wrote and some of my characters spoke, than the others—well, almost any new fiction book would be, excuse me. But that they'd maybe recognize that and do something entirely imprudent and unusual, like a shake-up with the award. But why Buckley's? If Pond's was tinsel and stocking-stuffer stuff and the currently correct attitude on all things political and every now and then what comes off as serious head-thinking culled from other writers' ideas—as if fiction should be intelligent and intellectual and anything but emotional and obsessed with people suffering and work and death. Hey, I think I made me there a statement, and even one reasonably close to what I believe. But her book, on the other hand—Buckley's—was just pure old story and bad prose and puff, written in lipstick passing as blood." "You read it?" and he says "That one I only gave a good look to, and by now I'm a pro at quickly flipping through, and after a ho-hum half-hour I found it to be utter junk and maybe the clunkiest of the bunch," and Ned says "Give it another half an hour and see if it doesn't bite, for a lot of people, I'm afraid me included, would beg to differ with you. But how do you feel, not that I can't tell and haven't heard, but for the paper tomorrow when we run our annual article on the awards ceremony and in particular that our hometown boy lost?" and he says "Sure, if you want. How do I feel? Disappointed, I suppose, how else? Though surprised and extremely grateful my book got this far in the—" and Ned says "We can't use the surprised–extreme gratitude line, as we already quoted you on that right after you heard you were a finalist," and he says "Then this then, and I'm not reading it off anything either, but it's suddenly so perfectly formed in my head it may seem that way," and he reads off the slip of paper he also has Ned's phone number on and notes for a five-minute acceptance speech all the finalists were asked to prepare. " 'Losing will keep me lean, mean and edgy, so in the right fighting weight and shape and mental and reflex condition for writing more. Winning would only have put me into tuxes and tight shoes and suits and on the speech and interview circuit for two years and judging a lot of lackluster writing awards and turned me into an overfulfilled sluggard and softie.' That should do it, no?—because how much could you want from a loser? But please don't put any of the other things I said in, as I don't want to sound like a lousy sport," and Ned says "Got you, and thanks for coming out and calling. Oh, which reminds me, how are the accommodations there? All you finalists get together for a snappy brunch or some good lobby or elevator-waiting conversation?" and he says "Ah, my publisher didn't put us up at the Plaza like the others did for their writers, I understand. But he said he'd take care of our continental breakfast and the hotel sitter for the kids tonight so long as the four of us slept in two double beds in a single room. It's okay by me, I don't feel I'm missing out on much, except the better breakfast, and I never was one for schmoozing, and the guy's barely got enough dough to cover our five-hundred-dollar table tickets here and get him and the editor back to Minneapolis. Though if you don't mind, please don't quote me on that either. Really, nothing except what I gave you, and that we've had a wonderful day taking in the museums and bookstores, one of which even had a copy of my novel, and are now having tons of fun despite losing—or maybe because of it. You see, my wife and I look on ourselves as renegades here or, better yet, barbarians let through the castle's gates for the day, though of course where we have to sleep outside its walls tonight in the cold. Nah, melodramatic and literary allusive, so please don't use any of the last stuff either," and Ned says "It's your day, pal, so if I'm able to sort out what's usable and not I'll cross out everything but what you want to say."

He goes back to his table. Main course is at his place. "Cold now," his wife says; "maybe we can ask one of the irascible waiters for a whole new plate." She's eaten what she's going to eat of hers. "What is it, lamb, veal, pork, even a beef chop?" and she says "What'd you tell Ned?" and he says "And the sauce—did it look like that when they first set it down?" and she says "Looks congealed but it isn't—it's good, if you feel like eating," and he says "Usual humble fare. How the best man obviously won, since it's obvious, because he won, that he was the best man. And, you know, that I feel fortunate to have got this far in the award process, though I think I said 'lucky,' and with such a long book and little publisher and few reviews and really no ads anywhere," and she says "Didn't he write that up in the article he did of you when you were nominated and in almost those words?" and he says "So he'll remember and won't use it, or he won't remember and we'll both look like fools to the few readers who do remember, or he'll just replace it with something comical and acute I didn't say, because it'll look better for me or the article if I did. Did say it, I mean. But hey, we're supposed to be having a good time here, kicking up a storm, alienating the aristocracy. And what's the difference anyway? For now that I've lost, the book's a dead egg. No, dead eggs you can still scramble or poach, so it's just flat-out dead, period, literally an unrefrigerated hundred-year-old egg even Chinese gourmands won't eat," and he looks at the publisher, smiles and says "Having a good time? I know I am," and the publisher nods and motions with his wine glass as if someone just made a toast, and drinks, and Rob beams at his editor, and she says "Too bad they have no music. If they did I'd ask us all to get up and dance, even in a circle, holding hands, in the folk dance manner," and he says "So we'll drink and horse around instead, laugh so hard the other stiff tables will look at us with indifference," and holds up his filled wine glass and says to her and the publisher "Till next year with a new work, okay? You both still game?" and the publisher says "What? I didn't catch that, Robert," and he says "Next year with a new book of mine, what do you say?" and the publisher says "Why not. You nearly broke me this year with this affair, though with all the publicity we stand to make some returns, so I'll be further broke next. Because I'm having great fun. All you nominees reading last night, the dinner tonight, meeting other publishers when I could never call myself one till this month, it's all been marvelous. Yes, we'll all come back next year, same writer, same award, same time, even the same table—number six—write that down, Sissie," and the editor says "I recorded it up here," pointing to her head, and the publisher says "With too much to drink, which I expect, we all might forget. But does Robert have a manuscript ready for us?" and Rob's wife says "Don't worry about this guy. Living is writing, writing is living, even the stomach flu along with a death in the family and cramps hardly stop him for a day, so expect one every year and only occasionally every other year, till you yell uncle."

The sitter's sitting in the semidark when they let themselves into their hotel room. She whispers "I suppose, because you didn't phone, that it wasn't good news. I'm very sorry, sir. My fingers were crossed, and I even recited a brief good-night prayer for you with the children. I hope you don't mind," and he says "Right, no news is no good news at times, and, for all we know, prayers work against me, but thanks. How were they—the kids?" and she says "Disappointed you didn't phone. They knew what it meant too and said things like they felt very bad for you, and I think for themselves a little also, since they said that if you won you promised to take them to FAO Schwarz tomorrow and give them each a twenty-dollar bill to spend. This week, one day after work, I'm going to look for your book in a bookstore, only I wish you'd be there to sign it for me," and he whispers "Here, and this is in addition to your wages tonight, take the one I read from yesterday," and asks her name and signs it "To Cecily Houston, who sat for us night this book lost the AFA, thanks and very best," and says "I haven't gone through it yet for typos, except for the pages I read from last night—580, nine down, 'north' instead of 'nouth,' 581, fourteen from foot, single quote mark before the double after the word 'slug,' but those I already wrote in when I was reading, plus a couple of commas for periods on those pages and the next and the word 'entrenchment' missing somewhere in the middle of 583. So I know there must be hundreds of corrections to be made, if not a thousand plus hundreds, which by all rights should foul up my sleep. The book, you see, first read in galleys by the judges of the award, was hurried into print early when the news of the nomination came out," and she says "Galleys, like ship kitchens? I don't understand," and his wife says "Shh, you two—the kids," and he whispers to the sitter "Really, it's not important, an asterisk to this whole silly shebang."

In bed his wife kisses his back, plays with him, and he says "I'm sorry, I just don't feel like it; imagine, *me*. But my mind's off somewhere, thinking about how I'd feel right now if I'd won, what I'd be doing and so on, worried about the morning and all the fuss and scurrying around me and arrangements being made and what I'd have to wear, even. Other than for the tux and old sports jacket and corduroy pants and single shirt and tie, I didn't come prepared for that," and she says "So you'd buy, for you get a ten thousand dollar check with the prize," and he says "It takes me days to decide, and I could buy clothes so early in the morning? Because they'd probably want me for some network or local 'Today'-type show around eight or nine. But would've been nice, no? Winning, I mean—fooling around with you too, of course—but also rejecting all that comes with the win, or most. 'Sorry, but each appearance I make takes away about two pages of my new manuscript.' 'Sorry, but you can't keep my fountain pen, nor will I sign

the photocopy you made of my story; it does something to the nib.'
'Sorry, but I truly feel I've been overinterviewed'—'prodigally,
immoderately' (I'd switch it around a bit)—'supererogatorily, in
excess of and over and beyond and above the call of blathering and
dry cleaning my clothes,'" and she says "I can understand it. I'm a
little sloshed myself from the evening's excess. Did you take aspirins?" and he says "Aspirins and Alka-Seltzer. I bought some
packs, knowing I'd drink and think too much, before we left yesterday. It's probably been on the eleven o'clock TV and radio
news already and in the newspapers—at least the articles have
been written—and certainly over the news service wires. It could
even be in the *Times* edition just hitting the streets, if there's one
between the city and late editions. I want to read about it tomorrow. I don't, really, but I don't want to duck around it either.
Good, I didn't win; life will be easier and my work harder. Pond,
what a yuk. I wonder what he's doing now. Probably entwined in a
phone-off-the-hook all-time celebratory screw with his wife, even
if they haven't done it in years, let's say. Sure they have, in that
period of time just about everyone their age does, but this is a special night—brain's burning and blood's burbling and nerve end-
ings are especially trembling. Or they could still be at the champagne reception at the Plaza. We could probably still be there too,
but after ten minutes of it you also had enough, didn't you? I
never really asked. But talking elatedly with three people at once.
And taking in with characteristic modesty for such an occasion the
last congrats of the judges and AFF officials and some high-born
or just gold-crusted AFF benefactors who forked over thousands
to be at this fete, and maybe even some publishing brass—almost
certainly his own—who tomorrow can go into work late. All of
them, though, slobbering and sucking all over him. It's the new
Pond dance, everyone's doing it. Or maybe he's being prepared
this very minute by a Sklosby publicity exec as to how to appear on
TV tomorrow on one of those early morning news-and-nothing
programs or midmorning-crisis talk shows. How to smile, how to
look serious—no, he's dour enough, so could teach them. But
how to hold back on your remarks till the interviewer has made his
full range of compliments about your book without having read it.
'Though don't fidget with your wrists or toupee,'" and she says
"His hair's real—thick with not a bald spot or single gray," and he

THE VICTOR

109

says "Well, to me it looked that way, all of one piece, or maybe I'm thinking of his writer's beard, which looked pasted on. 'But stare straight at the camera, Lem, and try not to move your head erratically and, for certain, don't curse, even if the blips will cover it—lots of people can read lips. In fact, curse, though not big curse words, for the audience might think you're looking down your nose at it. Oh, just be yourself, Lem; call the moderators by their first names, let them call you what they like, though don't blink too much or spit. In fact, be yourself completely. Blink, belch, patronize, boast, butt in and spit. That's what the home folks want from a writer—the real thing. Even have a parrot on your shoulder and come in drag.'" "Really," she says, "go to sleep if you're in no mood for making love. I thought it would help relax you, I still think it would, but maybe you can use the rest more," and he says "It would have helped and of course be enjoyable, but I'm just too sour to. Too full of drink too, too keyed up. Too everything. Too eager to get back to my writing after two days. Too many aspirins and antacids in me too. Too pissed too, with rotten anger and revenge, the too-too creeps. I never should have gone to that stupid gala, squeezed myself into that plastic tux and those steel shoes. But boy am I going to dish it out to them now. My own publisher won't even want it," and she says "Shh, shh, sweetheart," and kisses the back of his head, turns over on her other side, and he turns over on his side to face the back of her, fixes the covers on them, moves up to her, and they start making love.

Way it didn't happen. Chairperson says " . . . is Robert Bermmeister for his novel *Scorch*, published by . . . " "I can't believe it," he says to his wife, kissing her. "I can't believe it, this is impossible," he yells to the table. The editor's hugging the publisher. She jumps out of her chair and runs around the table to Rob and hugs him. "Do you believe it, do you believe it?" he says to her. "I mean, being a finalist was more than enough, right? But this, it's crazy, how'd we do it?" and she says "You deserved it, silly," and he says "Ah, those blessed judges, I could kiss them all." The publisher's stretching across the table to shake his hand and can only reach his elbow and squeezes it. "Stand, Robert, stand," and he says "Me?" and the publisher says "Sure, you, you have to go up there and make a speech and take your bows," and he says "Me, a speech? I didn't think I'd win. This is ridiculous, I've never been so happy," and he stands, waves to the applause, yells to his wife "What do I do, what do I say?" and she says "Whatever you want to, it's your moment, though just be nice," and he says "You're right," kisses her, turns to the editor to kiss her and is blinded by the spotlight, shields his eyes, a voice from the podium says "Come on up here to be officially congratulated and to accept your statuette and check, Robert, please come up, as you're also delaying the entrée," and the crowd laughs, and two young women, probably AFF workers, take his arms, one says "Follow us, sir," and they escort him around the tables to the stage, people seated and standing pat his back, arms, someone musses his hair, and he looks at the guy and doesn't know him but smiles at him, grab his hands as he passes, say "Wonderful," "Congratulations," "Bravo, Robert," "Glad you got it, terrific book," he turns to some of them and recognizes no one, keeps smiling, is near to crying, reaches the stage, woman holding his right arm says "There are four steps altogether, Mr. Bermmeister, and they're awfully steep, so be careful," and he says "Thanks, got a cane? Only kidding, thanks very much," and they let go of him, and he walks up the steps and over to the podium, shakes the chairperson's extended hand, hand of the president of AFF, two other people's, all four say "Congratulations, Robert," the president gives him the statuette and check and says "When they're done applauding, please say something," and Rob steps up to the mike, looks out, bows, waves, too many lights, wants to see his wife but can't make her out, glasses are wet, dries them with a handkerchief, they're stained now and even worse to see out of than before, breathes hard on the lenses and then rubs them on his jacket sleeve, applause is dying down, looks up, smiles, puts the check away, takes the paper with notes out of his pocket and holds it below the podium and reads it, nothing he can use and has to remember to call Ned sometime in the next hour, what's he going to say now? Just thanks to everyone and get off of here, looks up, sees his wife, and she waves at him, he blows a kiss to her, "That's my wife I did that to, I want you to understand," people laugh, then the room's quiet except for some buzzing, flash bulbs, cameras clicking, ice in glasses tinkling, everyone's seated, and he says "Thank you. Really, thanks. Everyone. I can't believe this," holding up the statuette and patting the jacket pocket with the check, then realizes they wouldn't know what that means. "I mean, I'm beginning to but it's still hard. That's what I yelled when I first heard"—can't come up with her name—"the chairperson say my book won; how it couldn't be possible. I thought anyone else but me. They were all so deserving. Each of the other four finalists deserved it and, in my mind, more so than I. It's true; it's what I thought. You can ask my wife; she's honest to the core and wouldn't lie about this for me. So this is all so maddeningly surprising, really. Not maddeningly; it's just crazy, crazily surprising and silencing, beyond words. I didn't, as you see, prepare a speech because I didn't expect to win, honestly. In fact, if any of you saw me peeking at a piece of paper below the podium before, it was my losing speech if anyone was going to ask me for one. It's the truth, or sort of. I prepared it for the book review editor of the *Boston Globe* who wanted me to call, win, lose or draw, or if somehow the foundation had made a mistake by listing me as one of the finalists. I won't read it now, self-ridiculingly funny as it might possibly be, because it'd be too absurd to," and someone shouts "Go, read it," and he says "No, thanks but no, I'd rather fail at extemporization than at preparedness," and some people laugh and applaud. "Does that mean I'm through or should be? Anyway, before I go let me just give my thanks. I know I'm only supposed to have five minutes to speak, and I've already blown a couple of them. So my deepest thanks to my wife, my kids, my mother for her encouragement, my father, may he rest in peace, for giving me the necessary discouragement I think every writer needs to keep him going with his work, and also a sense of humor and lots of stories. My mother again for encouraging me to read, for knowing all the words when I didn't, and during my early writing years and later ones too—I just didn't want to give my dad more praise than her, in what I said before—for never giving up on me, always encouraging. And the publisher, of course, Lawrence Terngull, and my editor, Sissie Lassner—please, she should take a bow. Without her I doubt the book would have been published and she even designed the cover and did the layout and everything like that. She's at my table; please, if you could get the light on her," and a spotlight finds the table, there's applause, she stands, waves, blows a kiss to him with both hands. "And Jeffrey Baker for loaning me his tux, Pic 'N Pay, or is it Pick and Pay? for having black dress shoes for twelve bucks, which I'll probably only wear this one time in my life. And finally the, well, my wife Jane again, though I could never say enough about her, all of it nice. And I said the publisher, but for backing this agentless worstselling author and especially in so large and expensive a book to produce. And the typesetters or printers or whatever they are and also the copyreader and proofreader for having to deal with those endless paragraphs and oddly constructed sentences and intentional misspellings and such. And finally the judges, the foundation, all of you for coming here, and the manual typewriter, erasable paper and pencil eraser, and Mr. Cavalieri, the one person in Boston who's still able to fix my aging typewriter and find the parts. Thank you, I'm so happy I can't tell you how much," and steps back from the podium, is applauded, shakes hands with the four people on stage, "Very nice," "Very natural," "A shot in the arm to all of us," "Congratulations again, Robert," leaves. As he's going down the steps he thinks why didn't he can all that thanks crap and mention that writer who's in hiding because of the Iranian death threat he's under for his book? Just to say "Don't forget, besides the monstrous horror against him, it's also an abomination against all culture and civilization, we should do something about it, all we can, keep writing and speaking out and using whatever power we have and getting literary and all those kinds of organizations here to do the same thing against it and in every way possible pressure our government to do something, like a complete trade embargo and economic sanctions against Iran, if they're not the same thing, and other people and organizations of other countries to pressure their governments and labor unions and such and pressure the UN also till the sentence is lifted and the guy can do what the hell he wants with his life, like walk along the street again with his kid without thinking he's going to get stabbed or shot and the kid too," is escorted by the same young women to his table, back patted, slapped, arms squeezed, "Damn," he thinks, "that's what I should have said, plus a few quick start-off thanks, instead of rattling on so foolishly and self-depreciatively, what a chance, what a dud," hands grabbed and shaked till one time he almost drops the statuette, good, who needs the stupid ugly thing, and where's he going to put it anyway except in some out-of-the-way storage place so he can never see it again? Someone pops up in front of him, blocking his way, and says "Mind signing your book, Mr. Bermmeister? It'll take a second," and holds out the book and a pen and he says "You bet, and thanks for buying it," and the man says "You're welcome—actually, I didn't buy it, it was a book trade between your house and mine—we fielded one of the other finalists, Buckley's *Ye Who Enter Here*," and he says "Looks like my house got the best of the deal, since that was some book," and the man says "I'm not taking sides in this," and Rob signs his name and then says "Oops, I forgot to ask to whom," and the man says "Sally, and the date if you don't mind—November 28th," and he writes above his name "To Sally, via the fella who gave me the book to sign for you, best and thanx," and puts the date after his name and someone says "What're you doing, Robert, writing a short story?" and he says "Just an appreciative inscription—I at first thought he bought this too-expensive book—I'm only kidding," he says to the man and hands him the book back, gets to his table. "I hope he wasn't offended," he thinks. Spotlight's on the table, people crowded around, most of them reporters and photographers, judging by their equipment and clothes. "So how do you feel, Mr. Bermmeister?" one asks, and he says "Feel? Just great, what do you think? Great. Totally unexpected, winning it. What a bunch of writers to beat out. I mean, they're not really beat out. Their books are there to be read and revered—*reveered*, how do you say the bloody word?—for a long time, and it might take them a little longer, maybe because they're more complex, before they surpass my book's recognition. But my head's still swimming from the surprise and excitement of the announcement, so if you don't mind, nothing more than what I said up there till my head's cleared." He sits. "Oh boy," he says low to his wife, taking her hand and kissing it, cameras click, "this is too much—am I sure my fly's zipped up, I don't have drool on my lips?—I need a drink," and she hands him his glass, "I don't know why I didn't think I could get it myself," and she says while he's drinking "Go easy for now, and listen, get used to this, and tonight's attention will probably be the worst," main course is on all the surrounding tables and is now put before them, he's hungry and picks up his knife and fork when a reporter asks "What do you think of the food, Robert— taste any better now that you've won?" and he says "Food? Who can eat? And again, I'm so nervous and excited I'm afraid it'll go in my lap, ruining Jeffrey Baker's new tux and costing me a fortune to clean it or replace. He's a writer, by the way, who lives down the street from me," and a woman says "Mr. Bermmeister, sorry to interrupt your meal, though the kitchen will keep your plate warm—and all you newspeople if you wish—would you come to the Louis the Fourteenth room for a brief press conference?" and he says "Sure thing, I guess," stands, whispers to his wife "Where you think the losers go, the Sixteenth?" kisses her, then whispers "It is Louis Seize who got his head chopped off, in case I gotta make a joke, right?" and she nods, he follows the woman, in the corridor outside the ballroom he sees Pond from a distance and shouts "Pond, Lemuel, hi, it's me, I'm sorry, and I meant every word I said about you up there—you know—the rest of you and especially you," reporters take this down, he says to the one closest "Oh Christ, look at me, how does anyone like me win such an award? I can't even speak," and Pond waves without smiling, it seems, though he can't really tell because of his big beard, and goes into, he sees when the door opens, the men's room. "Doesn't look happy, I don't think," he says to the AFF woman. "Well, why would he be? I doubt I would be too." Goes into the Louis Quatorze room. TV lights go on when they enter. Two cameras, few microphones on a lectern, reporters, maybe twenty of them, and the AFF woman points to where he's supposed to stand and says "Ladies and gentlemen, Mr. Bermmeister," and he says "Heilo, thanks for being here, I hope I haven't disturbed your meal. Well, I'm ready for whatever from you, not that anything I say here will be the last word, meaning, that I really, in all this excitement again, haven't the wherewithal—not that, but the in-telligence, the thinking cap—*on*, you know—to convey any articulate statements and sentiments about anything but my painfully tight shoes and borrowed tux, but shoot. Not literally, but go ahead, I'm ready, and sorry for my silly jokes—feeble tries at them, rather," and a woman says "We understand, Robert, and we'll do our best to refine what you say if it doesn't come out well. You're still a bit overexcited, no excuses needed—so be as informal and as much yourself as you want," and he says "Though what I said before wasn't recorded, was it? Because if it was—," and she says "Don't worry. If it's on tape it won't be used and will be erased or destroyed—that's not what we're interested in," and he says "So what are you then? I mean—," and she says "Basically, from my standpoint, sir, in an abridged version of the acceptance speech

you made, since we only have so much air time for the story, and
some of us were setting up here and didn't get it for radio or TV.
And then some elaboration, if you will, and perhaps even in-depth
exploration to things pertaining to your writing and the award
that the other reporters might ask you and maybe even me too,
okay? Okay, let's start, for I'd love to get it on the eleven o'clock,
and I think some of the print people have deadlines of their own,"
and there's a pause, "Face the camera please, sir," and he does and
she makes some hand signals to the camera crew, then says "Mr.
Bermmeister, well, how do you feel about winning the award?"
and he says "Just what I said in there," pointing to the door, "I—"
and she cuts him off and says "I should have told you this, Bob.
Robert? How do you go by?" "Either." "Well, pretend it's the first
time you're saying it, so no 'just-what-I-said's' please or pointing,
since no one watching will know what you're pointing at," and he
says "Make everything seem as if it only just happened, which it
almost just did, but I got it. All right. I'm shocked, surprised—"
and she says "Wait'll I ask the question, Bob. Now," hand signals to
the crew, "Mr. Bermmeister, how do you feel about winning it?"
and he says "Surprised, shocked, very surprised, almost incredibly
so. Totally unexpected, and excited. It was unexpected, and I'm
excited because for me it was so unexpected, to the point where I
was made speechless. No, that's not exactly so. Moment it happened I yelled out 'It can't be,' or something like that. 'Impossible.
This is. Wake me up.' My wife would remember the exact words.
To tell you the truth, and I know I'm going on too much with this,
it was more than enough, although perhaps not to my publisher,
though he was quite ecstatic enough, though who wouldn't be and
particularly when your company's that small and new and never
had a major success, though we both thought that as long as I was
nominated and it was going to somebody . . . oh, where was I?
Lost my train of thought. You'll have to edit and splice, whatever
the term is, to make sense of this or just do it over. For I was saying
something about how being a finalist was more than enough for
my publisher and me, though as long as—" and she says "Let me
ask you this, and we're still running. Why are you so shocked and
surprised, as you said? After all the acclaim your book's received
so far, you don't believe it deserves the award?" and he says "What
acclaim? There was the nomination, of course, but almost no re-

views, though okay, it's only been out a month. Four, to date, and only one from a prepublication review service, so five altogether. We thought the nomination would generate more, though maybe that's what got us the four newspaper reviews. And of those, only two—possibly three, if I stretch the praise a little on that one and sidestep what can be construed as complaints—were good, but certainly not smashingly so. But you know, but you wouldn't, but it's almost always been like that, minus the nomination and award and two or three reviews, for all my books when they were published. Day of publication with those it was as if the publisher just dropped the book off the George Washington Bridge and you watched it sink. But if there was a passing barge or boat below— the rare chance of that happening, is what I mean, though which must've in this case—and it hit someone on the head, then maybe there'd be some attention given to it, like a feature news piece with the lead 'Book Beans Boatman,' or something. So what I'm saying is that other than for the nomination and now the award, and maybe the one fairly good review it got in my city and leap-from-nowhere articles that same paper gave me—but something like that's almost *de rigueur*, if you know what I mean: hometown always wants the hometown boy to make good, if he hasn't been insulting to it, for it looks good for the hometown—there hasn't been any acclaim. And does my book deserve the award, I think you asked? Who am I to say which book does? Maybe them all, and also some books that weren't nominated—certainly some of those—and I just got lucky, that's all, but it's probably more than that, though what, I don't know. Not that I'm disputing the judges' judgment, you understand. I'm grateful—eternally, or as far as that goes—I mean it, for something like this, if you know how to live with it, can't do anything but good for the book. And a real writer . . . ah, forget what a real writer thinks, says, how he acts, that kind of business, as if I were one. But you know, your book can win for the wrong as well as the right reasons. Maybe less chance of that happening with five judges, which is why they have that number, but every so often there can be a fluke there too. For someone can see something really good in it that wasn't intended, in or under the writer's mind, and if that person has a strong personality or persuasive delivery or is preeminent in his field or just famous for any reason, really, and the others aren't well known and are weak or just easily manipulated or swayed, this person can convince them this is there when it's not, and what do you do about that? Protest that someone raved about your work and then got the rest of them to, for the wrong reasons he saw into it or just said to show his power or ability to persuade or to test out how compelling his preeminence or fame is? I'm not being very clear, am I?" and she says "No no, it's okay, but—" and he says "When my sentences get too long, I lose touch with what I started out to say. There, that was a clear one and ended with a monosyllable, my favorite way. But I'm also too excited, surprised, since this award just happened, didn't it? And besides that, I've had nothing to eat since breakfast, and that wasn't much—toasted English muffin, margarine because they didn't have butter, and black coffee—for my publisher's been carting me around town all day signing books, a new experience for me and which I'm sure also came out of the nomination and possibility that I might win, and then I don't know—wait, here I go again with my long sentences—what the heck happened to lunch. Maybe—good, I stopped—maybe that was the English muffin and coffee on the run, and breakfast was just toast. And I also, at the cocktail reception just before the awards dinner, had, with just a couple of skimpy hors d'oeuvres—" and he suddenly sees his editor beside one of the cameras, waving her hand across her mouth for him, he thinks, not to say what he was going to and then making motions to drink several quick shots and shaking her head right after. "Well, like that," he says. "For being hungry and a bit tired, I have to admit—they really moved me around today—can make one, *me*, confused and nervous and thus inarticulate and unintelligible too." "Okay, that ought to do it," she says. "Thanks, Bob," and the TV lights go out, and another reporter, holding a pen and pad, says "What will you do now that you've won, Mr. Bermmeister?" and he says "Do? Finish my dinner tonight, but I know you mean something different. But I hardly started it, and I mentioned my hunger, so if my plate's still there, and probably—no, no doubt—call my kids and my mother and wife's folks to tell them I've won. I told them I'd call, but only if I won, so I also told them not to expect to hear from me. And I don't know, I guess there'll be some celebrations somewhere, at least where I teach, and oh yeah, and this is probably the most important thing—in ways, the only important thing in what

I'll do with the award . . . I wish, I'm not a publicity seeker but I wish the cameras were still on for this but that's okay, do what you want," and waits a few seconds for the woman TV interviewer to react but her back's still turned to him while she talks to another woman and the cameras and lighting equipment are being torn down . . . "Anyway, if it's possible, to use my win as a platform—I don't know if that's the way to say it—but for the novelist, the Indian living in England, on the lam, really, lying low, constantly guarded by English cops . . . oh, God, I suddenly forgot his name but it'll come, but the one the Iranian government and Islamic fundamentalists there . . . the mullahs . . . all, really, together, for you know, one doesn't operate without the other in that country, and both groups, religious and political . . . well, they're interchangeable and the same, aren't they? and both feverishly behind it . . . the ransom for his assassination, calling on every Moslem in the world, or at least of their sect—I mean, is that supposed to be religious?—and then not rescinding the call even after the guy—" and the reporter says "You mean, to use your platform to speak out against this threat," and he says "Yes yes yes, but not a platform, but what's his name? I feel lousy I can't come up with it. I mean, he's a first-rate writer, tremendous, one of the world's best, maybe not with that book, but that's not my point—but that also, my memory lapse with his name probably has to do with the excitement tonight and my hunger and tiredness—oh, I'm not making myself clear," and the reporter says "Don't worry about that. And about this writer, there already are, if I'm not mistaken, many well-known writers and writing organizations—the Authors League, for one—doing something along these lines. Though one more voice, and surely someone of your stature now, won't hurt the cause. But my question was somewhat more mundane than that. Will your publisher, because of your new stature, be sending you on the road with your book now that it's won? Any special appearances—TV, for instance—and do you think this attention will change you from the relatively unknown but hard-working, demanding craftsman you've been to someone whose new-found celebrity will stop him from getting to his work as much as he wants?" and he says "No question it won't. And my publisher's just a small guy so I doubt—small in the sense his house is; his publishing house; he's actually about six-four or -five—I doubt they have anything expensive planned for me like a book tour. But ask the editor there, Miss Lassner," and points to her and she says "We've lots of plans, lots. Rob has a great smile and disposition and has promised to be generous with his time for a short while, so it's a whole new ballgame now, I say happily," and another reporter says "Bob, you really don't use a word processor? For up on the stage before you said—the sound wasn't too good so I didn't catch it all—but about a manual typewriter," and he says "Manual, sure; tried and true. I like the keyboard action of it, what can I say? I'm like a pianist on my machine, banging out my anger and frustrations and such, not that that's what a pianist does—it's different, of course, and some of what I bang out's even positive. But it's what I learned on, though self-taught learned, and the word processor—three fingers, I mean, my typing, and if my left thumb's especially dexterous that day—or maybe it's the right," and he types in the air with both hands, "the left, then that thumb on the space bar. But the word processor—well you know, those things are complicated and cold, which'd take weeks out of my work to learn how to use—months, forever. And with their justified margins and perfect print, well, looking so good on the screen it makes you feel your work's maybe that good too, so, illusions, things done before they're done, besides your eyes. But if I was starting out today, say—a kid just out of college, a newsperson like you, but your age and my sex, with nothing at the paper or radio or TV station but processors to work on, or even a semi-whiz at computers or electronics, so with some feel of what runs those things, well then of course . . . anyway, manuals are what I do and am used to, and they're also light and one piece, not three separate sections to sling over your shoulders when you travel and weigh you down, and I can even clean the keys myself, use the vacuum cleaner to suck up the dust out of the chassis, and so on," and other questions—"Why the title *Scorch*?" and he says "Because I didn't want to call it Bernard—the main character's given name," when the reporter looks confused, and the reporter says "What do you mean?" and he says "I would've said 'Christian' but he's not. Just kidding, I know what you asked, but you know, *scorch*, what the word reverberates—did I say 'reverberates'? 'Resonates' is what I meant—that everything in the book or just about goes up, is hot. Not sent up but that too in a way . . . it's supposed to be a fiery book, a dry, sizzling, burning, fast, even an excoriating book, but I'm also not very adept at explaining about myself or my work, just as I'm probably not at anything—explaining, I'm saying"—all of which are innocuous and slight and he feels he answers insufficiently and insipidly if sometimes stupidly because of his tries at humor or plain speech or eloquence with fancy words, and then the reporters thank him—not one thing did I answer right, he thinks, not one except maybe the title thing . . . no, nothing, which will make people think who see or read the interview or hear it on radio "This fop wrote that book? Not one I'm going to borrow or buy." A couple of them wish him good luck, and one says "Hope you make a killing," another, when the others are no longer near, says "Off the record, Bob, with your family and job and all the other chores every responsible adult has to do, how have you been able to write so much? I'm a novelist too, albeit not as successful," and he says "I just hack away at it but not like a hack, chip by chip if I have to, ten to fifteen minutes at a time lots of times plus a coupla weekend hours when my wife and I spell each other, and you can print that if you want," and the reporter says "No, that was just for me, thanks," and he returns to the table with the editor, apologizing for bringing her into it when he could see she didn't want to and for giving such a sappy interview, and she says "What are you saying? Any publicity is good publicity so long as you don't cuss out America too sharply or say you've a liking for little boys or girls. And yours was fine—your great smile, your words, one could see the serious writer's mind working—we must have sold another thousand copies from it," and he says "You can't mean that; I was a grade-A schmuck," and she says "Cross my heart and hope you get a *Sunday Times Magazine* article—it was real and informative. So, sold books or not, which isn't the goal, I do mean it; you'll be great on tour." He sits down, kisses his wife, says "It went lousy, a spoof if I'd been spoofing, a fiasco because I wasn't," breaks a roll, reporter pulls a chair up, sits down and turns on a tape recorder and says "Mr. Bermmeister," and he says "Really, just want to eat, and everything I have to say about my work is in the work and that sort of standard writer thing, and the rest of it should be—how I'm now feeling—on my face," and the reporter says "What I'd love are your spoken thoughts of how you feel tonight but not on a stage to a thousand people or in front of cameras and a dozen other newsmen, which become events and can alter the truth of what you have to say," and he says "Well, great then, I feel great of course, what do you think?" and the reporter's motioning with his hands "More, more," and he says "Humbled also—not humbled, that's bull, or at least for me, but something—but you see? I can't speak about these things. My wife can do it better for me than I can but she won't want to"—she's shaking her head. "Or my editor, publisher"—they're both waving him off—"or the waiter," and he grabs the arm of the passing waiter, who says "Your main dish, sir? We brought it back, but I'll bring it out now," and he says "No, yes, I mean, I'd like my food, I'm starving, but talk to this reporter, tell him what vintage wine we're having, how writers and their like probably tend to get smashed at these affairs—the free booze, lavish food, in the air all that perfume, the rich well-bred gentlefolk in their million-buck tuxes and skimpy gowns, fish that don't swim, clams that don't dry, jeez, what do you expect of us or at least me?—we're night-on-the-town, go-on-a-toot kind of guys, a day off from heavy construction work and whistling at passing girls, you could say, but who like to overdo the laboriousness of their labors and their commonplaceness and bad manners, as you can see, even when they don't win, if I'm making myself clear," and the reporter says "I think I got the message," and he says "Then you tell me," and the reporter says "You know. But this is still a good chance, Robert, for a small book. We go to a large number of educated people— it's public radio, syndicated—so good book buyers," and he looks at the editor, she's nodding, and the publisher, whose look and finger-pointing say "Anything she says goes," and he says into the mike "Okay, truth is, I am humbled, honestly, or at least feel small in comparison to the largeness of the honor. It's a fine thing to win, totally unexpected, a bigger shock than being nominated," the reporter's eyes are turned up to the ceiling as if this is all so trivial, "and I feel great about it. It may be the best moment of my writing life, in fact. Certainly the best thing that's ever happened to my work and maybe in the order of my personal thrills or whatever you want to call them—excitements, kicks, gratifications, fications, bliss—it comes after the birth of my first child, then the second, but I'm talking about when they happened, the baby suddenly out. Then my marriage ceremony and after that when my wife said she'd marry me and then when I first learned she was pregnant the first time and then the publication, rather the phone call from my first publisher saying they were taking my first book, which was actually my fifth or sixth book-length manuscript but the first to be taken. And the order that tonight's excitement comes in shouldn't be after the birth of my first but after them all, ending with the first book's acceptance and maybe even ending, and then comes tonight's, with the time I got a telegram from my U.S. senator—I didn't have a phone then, couldn't afford one— saying I'd won an N.E.A. grant in fiction when I'd given up getting any recognition or money for my work and was almost dead broke, and I think, for the first of several times in my life, about ready to give the whole writing thing up," and the reporter's smiling now, got what he came for, and says "That's wonderful, the twists life takes, then how things turn out; anything else?" and he's about to say something—how this award's particularly fulfilling, coming with a long complex book he didn't think anyone would take and being published by a small press—when a waiter sets down his plate, and he thanks him and points to his glass with an expression "Some more?" and the waiter signals with his fingers to someone and a waitress hurries over and pours wine into his glass, and the reporter says "So you were about to tell me something else, Robert?" and he says "I was going to say how rewarding the award is in other ways. For instance that it makes my mother and kids and wife and her folks so happy—it will, when they hear it. My wife, of course, sitting right next to me, has. In fact, my kids, oh my gosh, I forgot—excuse me but you have enough, don't you?—but watch what a good poppa I am for I gotta call and tell them I won before they go to sleep, otherwise they'll never forgive me," and his wife says "It isn't too late?" and he says "If it is, the sitter will say so, and really," to the reporter, "I also have to check up on the sitter to see she's working out all right," and leaves the room, foundation person is suddenly alongside and accompanies him, and he says "Really, you don't have to, I'll be right back, and what good am I in there anyway now? And they won't let you into the men's room, and I think I can find the phones—where are they," looking around the corridor, "you know?" and she takes him to a bank of them, stands a little off to the side, and he says "Really, this is personal and I tend to talk loud—I won't fly away—my wife's still there and our coats are checked," and she goes and he calls the hotel. "They're sleeping," the sitter says, "—no they're not, they're up, must've heard your rings or me talking," and his daughter gets on, "You win, Daddy?" and he says "Believe it or not, kid, I did," and she shouts "Piers, Daddy won, we can go to FAO Schwarz tomorrow, get up, let's celebrate—can we, Daddy?" and he says "Okay, for a moment. Tell the sitter, Miss Marlene, or I will, you can each have one of those overpriced cans of ginger ale in the little fridge—she too, but nothing else," and while his daughter's telling the sitter about the sodas and bag each of nuts or chips, "my father said so," his son gets on and says "I love you too, Dada, you have very good luck," and he says "I know, amazing; the babysitter nice?" and his son says "Very; she tells great stories," and he says "Good. Now kiss-kiss for the two of you from Mommy and me and don't eat all the chips or nuts right before sleep—bad tummy stuff—and put Miss Marlene on," and the sitter says "My felicitations, mister—we prayed for it here, the three of us in an innocent untheological way. Now it'll make it more troublesome getting them to bed again but, considering what caused it, it's worth it and we shall persevere and win—you'll be here by 11:30, please?" and he calls his mother, she says hello, and he says "It's me, Mom, Robert, did I wake you?" and she says "So-so, I could feel better. Anything wrong with you or your family?—it's so late," and he says "I did wake you then, huh?" and she says "No, I was dozing, what's wrong, the children okay?" and he says "I told you I'd call if I won," and she says "Won what?" and he says "The book prize," and she says "I must have forgot—for what?" and he says "My book, the novel, *Scorch*," and she says "The one you gave me? I love it. I'm going to start reading it tomorrow. I've been a little out of sorts lately to start it till now. But I show it to everyone every time they come here and they all think it's beautiful looking and it's so big, they call it a brick, everyone," and he says "Well listen, Mom, they had a contest—I'm saying, a gala, tonight, this foundation did, with an awards ceremony at the Plaza. I told you but you must've forgot, there were five nominees and, you know, I sent you articles about it—the *Times*, et cetera—and my book took first prize. Actually, the only prize," and she says "That's wonderful, you make me proud, all my children do. Now I'm a little tired, dear, do you mind?" and he says "I'm sorry, I didn't think it was so late—I'll call tomorrow, and we'll come see you next week and go out for lunch to celebrate," and she says "If I'm up to it, that would be nice." He calls his in-laws, and his mother-in-law says "It's been on the radio, darling, it's wonderful," and he says "So fast? It just happened, or almost. And Jane's okay, having a great time, and kids are fine, but, just out of curiosity, how did the newscast word it?" and she says "That you won this complicated award's name and the book's title—if you'd sneezed and someone quickly said 'God bless you,' you would have missed it," and in the background his father-in-law says "Offer Robert my own congratulations and tell him a friend's already called us and others are probably dialing now and that tomorrow I'm going to each of the bookstores here to see if because of this news any more copies have been sold. I've been watching the shelves and so far the same number of books have been there," and she starts to repeat it, but he says "Thanks, I heard." He calls the *Globe* reporter at home collect and says "First off I want you to know I tried charging this call to my home number, but the operator said I couldn't unless someone was there to vouch for me," and the reporter says "Don't fret, man, the paper phoned me the fantastic news, and I'm honored you even took to contacting me when you have to have so much else to do," and he says "You? You? The guy who made me and my publisher feel, till this big nomination deal came along, that the book was actually published once it came out? Come off it, we owe you tons," and the reporter says "Thanks, much too kind, but long as you did phone, I have twenty minutes to get the story in, which without your call would have been sort of a dead impersonal account of your win, so tell me how you feel," and he says "Still gratified and astonished beyond all measure, expectation and belief, and why? Because I was happily satisfied with just being a nominee, and I thought any of the other writers would get it, not only because of the high quality of their work and that they're much better known but also because I didn't think mine was that much or really even good enough to be published. But that's what I've thought about all my works when I finished them and they came out, so it's probably, in part, what I need to feel in order to start and then continue a new one," and the reporter says "You proved yourself wrong with this one, bub, but fine, you gave me exactly what I needed for the article. But on the lighter side . . . your tux and new dress shoes—you didn't feel, as you said you would, ridiculous and crippled in them?" and he says "Everything went perfectly—I even remembered how to tie a bow tie, and it's still in place," and the reporter says "Nice, nice, I like that. One quickie, Rob, and we're gone. Think the entire experience will change your life or even, that word you love to hate, your lifestyle?" and he says "Certainly—and hey, I'm getting good at this, aren't I? which is when I should start watching out—but certainly a prize of this magnitude would change the life of any writer who isn't dead, and I'll fight it every step of the way till I'm successful at not letting this new institutional success affect me. Because I'm not a speechmaker, prize-committee member—that's 'prize-committee' with a hyphen—organization joiner, panel or symposium participant or a spokesman for anything, including my own work. But if the prize does give the book a lot more sales and me, ultimately, the economic independence to do more of what I want to and maybe even a lighter teaching load for the same pay at my university, that'll be just dandy, for the only change I want in the style of my life is to find more time to read, think and write and spend more time with my family," and the reporter says "Couldn't be better—consider the article your first job ad," and he goes back to the table, plate's gone, desert's there melting. "Maybe at the hotel I'll room-service up a sandwich or steak," he says to his wife. "I can afford to do that one night in my life, can't I, even if I have to eat it in the bathroom, and what more deserving time than tonight?" and she says "Don't look at me to stop you," and he says "And champagne—not the little splits in the fridge but a whole big fancy French bottle if that cheap hotel's got it," and she says "Stick with the sandwich and maybe a good refrigerator beer." Later there's a reception for the nominees, judges, officials and heavy donors, he undoes his bow tie and lets it hang, and a photographer for a publishing trade journal says "Mind if I take you like that— it'll look like the fitting end to an emotionally and physically hard day," he is asked to sign several copies of *Scorch* that had been part of each table's center display, along with a gardenia floating in a bowl and a rusty tin cup of sharpened pencils and paper clips, his publisher says "Let's blow everything we're going to earn with your book and go to Elaine's for a nightcap and snack and chats with some of their famous literary clientele or at least a peek—

you're our entrée," but he says they have to relieve the babysitter, do, kids are asleep, has a sandwich sent up and has it with a couple of foreign beers, they make love, again early next morning, around seven the phone rings, it's the editor, "Just got a call they want you at a TV studio for national viewing, a limo could pick you up in half an hour, can you make it?" and he says "I've really nothing to wear but a smelly dress shirt and those wrinkled corduroy pants and old sports jacket I wore to those bookstores yesterday and the reading the other night," and she says "That's the costume—don't even splash water on your hair or brush it back till it's flat, we want you to completely look the part—only kidding . . . Mr. Terngull came with about a dozen shirts and pairs of socks so how about one each of his, though he's almost twice your size?" interview with a *Times* cultural affairs reporter later that day about his origins, antecedents, influences, aims with this book, future writing plans, feelings about his years of general obscurity and near poverty and now sudden recognition and perhaps wealth and fame, articles and profiles on him, book sells well, paperback, number of translations in a year, all his out-of-print novels and story collections republished in a unified edition, his school gives him a paid year off and tenure, and when he comes back he only has to teach one semester a year, gives readings around the country once a month at ten times what he got before, State Department tour through Eastern Europe and then Latin America, is invited to a literary festival in Japan, a symposium on the arts and censorship in Spain, is offered so much money to teach for a week at a summer writing conference that he can't turn it down, finishes the long short story he started before he got the award, plot's too melodramatic, language all wrong, has an agent now who sells it to a major magazine, thinks maybe he's not a short story writer anymore and should go back to what he did best or at least won him the award, starts lots of novels, tries writing plays, does an appreciation of a Norwegian writer he met at the Japanese festival and whose work he thinks just so-so but whom he's come to like and know and places it in a prestigious literary journal, on commission writes an essay on what it's like to be a cellar writer, as he calls it, and after so many years down there to suddenly come out into the light with a band playing and crowd waiting and much confetti thrown at him and applause and then, because this isn't his natural environment, to feel he needs to retreat back into his hole, it takes nearly four years to finish a short novel, which he does between travels, appearances, essays and reviews, his new publisher thinks it inferior to *Scorch* and a bit too short to publish alone, but they'll do it since they already paid him a sizable advance, while going over the copyedited manuscript he changes his mind about publishing it and returns the advance and tells the editor this novel isn't the right one to follow *Scorch*, which anyway maybe wasn't as good as he and lots of other people thought, "Maybe," he says, "just to change things around a little, the next one should be a collection of stories or essays," turns the novel into a short story, and the agent sells it, and no one he knows whose opinion he admires and trusts seems to like it, starts another novel, pecks away at it for years, puts it down, works on something else, takes it up, and so on, tries writing film treatments and scripts for lots of money but never gets the hang of it, possibly because he hates the restrictions and rules of the form and usually movies themselves, every so often reads an article about artistic prizes and what the big ones can do to the artist, some are able to overcome this ironic handicap and continue to grow in their work, most though repeat their old works or just don't produce much or at all and, if they still feel the compulsion to create, do so in related but less demanding fields, something dries them up, sometimes their family life breaks up, and occasionally the artist himself cracks up, psychologists and critics and scholars are asked about this and give all sorts of reasons and interpretations, "It's conceivable they only had one or two important things to say and only one or two original ways to say it, were fortunate to win the awards, and after that were afraid to parrot or parody themselves," "Why look at it as a negative phenomenon? Perhaps in the prize-winning work they felt they did it all and didn't see any point to continue creating, or just wanted an easier avocation, since art is hard," "It might be they don't think they deserve the acclaim and now feel sufficient guilt to stifle their work," "Fame works strangely and often unfathomably on the subconscious, for the good or bad," "It's possible the individual artist fears that once he's on top of his craft the critics will look for things to pick at or savage in his work that they never would have thought of touching on before, to bring him down a few pegs, for malevolent reasons, or because they think they're actually helping him and he's a big enough person now to take the assault or simply to ignore it," he thinks maybe they're all right, maybe only some are, though no two seem to agree with each other, tells his wife he wishes he could return to teaching full-time, for he just doesn't have enough to do the other eight months of the year, "Well," she says, "I'm sure it can be arranged."

THE
FALL

They've come back to the house after being away almost the entire day. Saturday, and she's—The kids and he, and they entered the house, he in the lead and carrying a big canvas bag filled with vegetables and fruits, and saw— They were away, first to the farmers' market. Good early start, did lots of things during the day, and when they got home, one of the kids yelling "Mom, Mom, we're back—" She didn't want to go. Said she was too tired and weak, and she looked it too, so maybe it shouldn't have been that much of a shock when they got home and— Usually she goes with them. All four in the car, fifteen-minute trip, every other Saturday unless the weather's bad. He'd wheel her around in the chair and she'd point or say she wanted to go to that particular stand and he'd push her there, and she'd carry in her lap some of the things they bought. The kids like the honey sticks they can find nowhere else but the Saturday farmers' market near where they spend a month every summer in Vermont. There's also an open-air bakery—three long tables together, with the sellers behind them—

where the kids like to get a croissant each, chocolate or plain, or a butterfly, though the French owner of what they call The Patisserie, though he makes all the goods at home, calls the pastry something else in French, but not *papillon*. They did that today. First honey sticks, which the kids finished. Then he got what he wanted from several stalls, asked the kids if they saw anything they wanted but pastries; they didn't so they lined up at The Patisserie, got two chocolate croissants and this time a walnut-raisin bread because he remembered last time they were here she said they should get one next time—they had too much bread in the house then to buy one—since she was sure she'd like it just by its looks. Apples, pears, cherry tomatoes, a canteloupe, cider, lots of different vegetables, three different kinds of greens, she likes steaming them, herbs—she gave him a list of which ones and which she likes to dry—"And if you can manage it, pick up a few small plants at the Gardenmobile for the side of the house, but tell the seller you want them mostly for the shade." At the Japanese grocer's, a single card table, half-pound of bean sprouts, daikon, strange kind of scallion—almost all white—and something that tastes and looks like Chinese parsley but the grocer's daughter—her father doesn't speak English—said it isn't. Then when they got home— Then they did lots of other things elsewhere and when they got home, each of the kids carrying a plant to show her mother and he a big bag of produce and the filled canvas bag— In the car after the market, before he pulled out of the lot, he said to the kids "So, where do you want to go now?" "Home," one said. "I want to show Momma the plant I chose." "For pizza," the other one said. "Yes, pizza, pizza," the first one said. "Too early for either," he said. "And lunch will be later. You had your honey sticks and there's half a croissant each if you want, and if you're still hungry after that there's pears, apples, carrots." "I'm thirsty," one said, and he said "You both had different kinds of cider samples—apple, apple-raspberry—at the fruit stand. What do you say we go to the art museum? It's a little chilly out, and it shouldn't be crowded so early." "Yes, the museum," she said. "Great idea, Daddy. I want to buy a Monet key ring I saw there. I've my own money I brought." The other wanted to buy one too and had money. They went to the museum, straight to the gift shop. It'd run out of Monet key rings and also Monet crayon sharpeners, their second choice of what they remembered from their last visit there. Everything else they wanted—a stuffed Paddington Bear, a doll based on a book about a girl, Linnea, who goes to Monet's garden, a multicolored Slinky —they didn't have enough money for, and he didn't want to add any to what they had, since he found the dolls and Slinky overpriced. A traveling Monet exhibition dominated the museum— he'd thought it left—and you needed special tickets for it. His would be expensive, theirs half-priced, and they'd seen the show two months ago, but what the hell, he thought, the kids like to take the audiophone tours—they didn't last time here but had since at two other museums, both plugged into one cassette and the youngest, it seemed, always darting the opposite way the oldest was going and pulling her plug out—and Monet was one of his favorite painters of any era, and tickets to the exhibition included admission to the museum. But they were sold out. "Well, long as we're here let's go in anyway; maybe we'll discover something new and there's always some of the permanent stuff we like." He bought tickets—the youngest girl's was free—and they walked around but there wasn't much to see if you didn't like, and he didn't, American colonial and Georgian furniture, vases, silver, an exhibit of teapots from around the world, second-rate eighteenth- and nineteenth-century European paintings and sculpture, the same room of African and New Guinean folk art, old drawings in a cramped space, two rooms of photographs of tiled roofs. Almost the entire Impressionist wing, which he felt was the only reason to come here if there wasn't a special exhibition he wanted to see, had been sent to another museum in partial exchange for the Monets, and the rooms had been temporarily converted to an expensive Parisian café resembling one in Monet's time, and the room where American contemporary art used to be had been turned, since they'd seen the exhibit, into a Monet gift shop. "Success, that's all, they're making a fortune," he said. "We got to remember to tell Mommy about this." "Maybe we can get the key rings in there," his oldest daughter said, but they weren't allowed in without a Monet-exhibit tag. They left the museum, but right outside it he said "No, I'm going to protest, this is too much," and went to the ticket counter and said he'd like passes for another day for the money he paid to get in today, and if they don't do that, then a refund. "I'm telling you, I've never done this before, but I feel shortchanged.

Outside of the Monets, which we couldn't get in to, this place is bare." After some discussion between themselves and then a phone call to someone higher up, the ticket sellers gave him three passes. "So what are we going to do now?" he said when they got back to the car. "Pizza," both kids said. "Okay, it's around lunch time," and they went to a pizza shop nearby, and he had coffee while they had pizza, garlic bread and, though he didn't want to get it for them because it's such junk but it was the only kind of drink for kids they had, soda. At the table he said "So what do we want to do after this—any good suggestions?" "Let's go home," one said. "I want to show Mommy the plant I chose and tell her what you said we should about the Monet shop before we forget," but he said it was too early. He'd made an arrangement with her. He'd take the kids all morning and half the afternoon if she gave him half a day free tomorrow. "I don't know what I'll do with them, if you want us to be out of the house," she said. "I can't drive anymore, so I can't take them anyplace. Maybe we'll cab some-where, and I'll work it like that." "If you don't think you can do it, or you'll get too tired, just give me a couple of hours in the morn-ing. That seems to be when you're strongest, and anywhere you want—here, outside—and I'll take them for the afternoon," but she said no, she'll figure something out. "And you know, it's not as if I'll be getting any of my important work done today. A few pages of reading, but the writing stuff I'm already too bushed to." Maybe by now, he thought, she isn't tired anymore—took a nap, got some rest—and she can get some writing in. Then she'll really think his giving her almost the whole day free went to something, and she'll do her best to give him more than two hours tomorrow, or at least those two. "Let's go to the playground," he said. "Too cold," and he said "So we'll run around and warm up and go down the slide and things. Come on, only a short time, and then we'll go someplace like the Bagel Nook for dessert, and even—I shouldn't be doing this; don't tell your mother; nah, no conspiracies, so tell her if you want—but another soda, though between you, and Soho brand this time, you know, only natural and no sugar." "Okay," "Yea." They went to the playground. He caught them at the bottom of the slide a few times, went down with each of them once, then the two of them in front of him, sprinted around the park the playground was in, then said he wanted to work out on the parallel bars—"Haven't done it in a long time and I like the feeling it gives my arms and chest after, puffs them up, makes them feel young." So while they climbed on the Junglegym, he went on the bars, just swinging back and forth while he stayed stiff between the bars and a couple of times flipping himself off and landing on his feet a foot from the bar ends. Then they sat in the car till he wasn't sweating anymore, and he said "Okay, dessert," and at the Nook he gave in and they got a soda each but the Soho brand and a plate of cookies and he had a coffee and buttered bagel. He thought of calling her to see how she was. "Should we call Mommy?" and they said yes and he said "Nah, now that I think of it, she's probably working and getting to the phone will be difficult for her," and the older one said "She always has her portable phone with her in her walker basket," and he said "Even still," for what he didn't want was to give her an excuse to tell them to come home, for, even if she doesn't get any work done, longer he stays away, more she'll feel she has to give him those two-hours-plus tomorrow and maybe even doing most of the putting-the-kids-to-sleep tonight instead of him. "So what now?" he said when they finished eating, "we still have some time left," and the oldest said "Let's just go home, Daddy; we've been out plenty," and the other said "That's right." "Why? I'm still feeling energetic and want to stay out and do things, and you must be feeling frisky too what with those two sodas and pizza and you finished the cookies, I see, and they looked good and sweet," and the younger said "They were okay." "Good. There are no movies you two would like," and the older one said "Why not?" and he said "Too violent or explicit or just plain disgusting," and one of them asked and he had to explain "explicit": "Where they show adult things kids shouldn't see and maybe not even adults, because they are so disgusting and, and . . . well a whole bunch of other words I'd have to explain, and the movies for kids are all stupid, just plain stupid." "Not all," the older one said, and he said "I meant most," and she said "Then let's go to the Rotunda. They have a good kids' bookstore there." He didn't want to, been there twice already this week getting things for the house and his wife, but it was a small fairly attractive mall, fifteen minutes away, so that would take time, and the ten to fifteen minutes back, and he could have another coffee at one of the two food places there while they had something, or nothing—

no coffee for him and they could just look at the books in the store and maybe each could buy one if that didn't come to much, and he could do a little supermarket shopping there so he wouldn't have to do it Monday or Tuesday, so he said "Yeah, that's a very good suggestion; I didn't think of it; thanks, dear." "I thought of it too but didn't say it," the younger one said, and he said "So thank you too. Maybe your sister picked it out of your head you were thinking it so hard," and the older one said "She's only saying that; it was my own." They went to the mall, kids to the children's bookstore while he browsed through the adult one across the hall and bought a book his wife had said she wanted weeks ago—a week, anyway—if he was ever near a bookstore. He had been—this one; in fact, several times since she'd said it, or a couple of times, at least—but he forgot: the new *Consumer Buying Guide* annual; "That or the one Consumer Reports puts out," which the store also had, but it was more expensive and didn't seem to have as much. She wanted to replace their broken-down drier and was also looking into buying a minivan, then selling the two-door they have, because it would be more comfortable for the family and also because of all the accessories she has to take with her when they go out: this elaborate Swedish walker with a basket and seat; wheelchair sometimes when they go to places—museums, theaters, zoos and parks— where she has to do a lot of getting around; eventually a motorized cart, she suspects, which means a special lift or removable ramp. "Just looking ahead," she said, "not deceiving myself, and a couple of companies—Chrysler, I know—are giving a five-hundred-dollar rebate on the lift, and I don't know how long that'll last. Maybe the response will be so great, or just nothing, that they'll cut it off." Older child found a book she'd always wanted, other one didn't see anything she liked. "Good," he said, "you did it right; didn't see anything you liked, you didn't buy. You're not, as they say, a compulsive shopper." Explained "compulsive" and said all this while they walked to the supermarket inside the mall, older child already reading her book along the way. Milk, yogurt, cheese, pasta, cabbage and beets, because he forgot to get them at the farmers' market and his wife wants them to make borscht, some cleaning things, wax paper, bread for the kids, deli, seltzer in several flavors, juice concentrate. "Can anyone think of anything we need but didn't get?" and the younger one said "Parakeet seeds, we're all out," and he said "Great; I'll tell Blue you reminded me, and will he ever be appreciative. Also those treat sticks as a special treat after the bread he had to eat the last few days." "And a light for my night light," the older one said, and he said "You still need that thing?" "Yes, and Mommy said the little bulb in that little lamp by her bed went out too, so we can get them at the same place." Got them, paid, when he was pushing the cart to the exit he looked at his watch. Why not give her another half-hour? More he gives, better rested she'll be. Probably rested plenty already and maybe only now is just starting to work. Even if she only gets a half-hour in, it'll be something, might satisfy her. "Mind if we stop someplace for coffee?" he said after he got the packages into the trunk. "I don't want to," the older one said. "We want to go home," the other one said. "Please, I'm a little tired; I could use a quick pick-me-up like a coffee." "You'll get sick with all that coffee," the older one said. "Mommy said you shouldn't have so much, and you get too angry with it too." "Not angry; nervous. But just now I need one. Sometimes an adult body does. I'm telling you, I know. And then with it, I won't be too sleepy to drive." So they went to a convenience store on the way home. He had a decaf—poured it himself when they weren't looking, not that they'd know the meaning of the red handle of that pot, but they might ask; they shared a fruit drink and a packaged pound cake. "Listen, whatever I said before about no conspiracies, this time please don't tell Mommy about all the cake I allowed you today. She'll kill me." They sat in the car in front of the store; then, to stop them from eating and drinking so fast, which when they were done they'd want to go straight home, he decided to start a conversation. "So, what did you both like best about today?" "It's not over," the older one said. "I know, but so far." "The pizza and soda." "Yes," the younger one said. "Besides that," and they both said the outdoor bakery at the farmers' market. "Seriously, what else? Not just food," and the older one said "The gift shop at the museum even if it didn't have my key ring." "I liked it when you went down the slide with us and then with me alone," the younger one said. "Now you're talking," he said. "I liked it all but maybe the slide, going down with you two together, the most. That was like heaven, but the good heaven, where you're alive—sliding down, my two darling girls in my arms in front of me. And it was also scary, we went down so fast." "Yeah, maybe that was the best," the older one aid. "And then the pizza and after that the French bakery." Then they went home. Opened the door. The older girl did; he had two bags of groceries in his arms and was going to go back for more once he put these down in the kitchen. The older girl screamed. The younger one, behind him, yelled "What?" and squeezed past him and ran in, and then she screamed. He went in with the packages; they were both already beside his wife on the floor, plants they brought in, next to them. Her eyes were closed; are closed; blood all around her head and arm but not coming out of the gash in her head anymore. He puts the bags down on the dining room table near her, says "Oh no, oh God," and yells "Go away, go away," and they get up and jump back and start screaming, and he gets on the floor and says to the ceiling "What am I going to do, what am I going to do?—stop screaming, I can't think," and they stop and he puts his ear to her mouth. She doesn't seem to be breathing. Turns her over on her back and puts his ear to her chest, to her mouth and nose, doesn't hear or feel anything. Feels her wrist but isn't sure he'd feel anything even if there is a pulse there, since he doesn't know how to do it. He breathes into her mouth, hard, pulls away, breathes some more, pulls away, says to the older girl "Call Emergency, 911, tell them your mommy's very hurt, unconscious, and to send an emergency ambulance right away. Right away. 911 and that she might not be breathing. Do it now, now," and bends down and breathes into her mouth and calls her name after he pulls away, breathes some more into her and calls her name again and again. "Oh why did I stay away, why didn't I come back?" he screams. Her walker's on its side. She must have slipped while pushing it and fallen, and the walker slid away from her and hit something and fell over, or she just slipped and fell with it and hit her head hard on something, not the floor, or maybe just something sharp on the floor, because of that deep gash. Later she'll say she doesn't know how it happened: she was getting out of a chair, had her hands on the walker for support, and that's all she remembers of it. "A towel, get a towel," he yells to the younger girl, "and wet it good so we can wipe Mommy's head —maybe that'll help her—and did you call that 911?" he yells to the older girl and she says "Yes, they said they're coming, they wanted to speak to you, but I said you were blowing air into

Mommy. Is she going to die? Is she dead?" and he says "No, never, don't think of it, go outside and wait for the ambulance and tell them this is the house. Wave to them, make sure they see you," and the younger girl's brought the towel, and he wipes his wife's head and face with it and breathes into her mouth, feels for her heartbeat, nothing seems to be there, breathes into her again and listens for her breath, nothing, calls her name, shakes her shoulders, yells "When will they come?—call them again—you," to the younger girl, "dial 911 and give them our name and address and say we called before and ask when they're coming," and she does. The emergency team comes about ten minutes after his older daughter first called them, and they put some machines on his wife and revive her, and he puts his hand on her temple and feels the pulse, and they say she probably never stopped breathing, it just must have seemed that way to him because her breathing and heartbeat were so low or he wasn't listening or feeling at the right places and that his mouth-to-mouth resuscitation probably helped rather than hurt, though sometimes it can do the reverse. She's taken to the hospital. When she goes she's smiling at them and muttering something they don't understand except for the word "outside." He leaves the kids with friends for a couple of hours and goes to the hospital. She's sleeping but not in a coma and will most likely be her old self tomorrow though with a tremendous headache, the doctor tells him. Then he picks up the kids, goes home, brings the rest of the bags in from the car, has to throw away a few things that spoiled, like milk and deli meat, makes them supper and himself a drink and sits down at the table with them.

MOON

One last one. To the moon. Goes outside, first leaves his wife in
bed. She was reading while he was reading, fell asleep with her
glasses on and holding the book to her chest. He took the glasses
off, book away, held her head while he took out the pillows it had
been against and laid them flat and rested her head on them. Two,
she likes to sleep with; he, one. Then shut the light and went outside. Has no clothes on. None needed. Kids sound asleep—he
knows, for he told them a story, then sang to them till they fell
asleep and sat ten more minutes in their room drinking his drink.
House in a remote area, not even lights from other houses can be
seen, and they almost have a 360 degree view of the hills around
them, valleys, and so on. Way off, maybe five miles, a lighthouse
light in the bay below. So: naked, nice out, cool but not so cool that
he's cold, more than a week before they have to leave this rented
house, little breeze, sound of insects—crickets, cicadas, one of
those, maybe another—sound of breezes through trees, every
now and then loons in the lake about a mile away, which he can

now see only because it's moonlit. So he's outside and looks up at the moon. Full face, no hair, nice face, cloud suddenly on top of it like a cheap toupee, toupee blown away. Then face way he best likes to see it: open and clear. Moon, he thinks. I've never really spoken to you. I still haven't. "Moon, I was just now thinking," he says, "I've never really spoken to you before, never have at all that I can remember, and my memory's pretty good, very good, nobody I know has a better one, so I haven't spoken to you, period, far as I can remember, at least not aloud. So what do I want to say to you? What was I leading up to with that long intro? Something, that I know—way you light up the night and how good it looks and makes me feel? Maybe that but much more. But it's so bright tonight I can almost read out here from your light. If I had a book with me, which I left on my bed. Not that I would read; I'd just look and at anything but the book if I'd brought it along. Anyway, what do you say to what I just said? Any to all of it, just that I want to speak to you but really, though I thought I had something, don't know what to say. Silly, I know, or another word, but if you can, do." Waits. "I'm serious, I'd love an answer from you of any recognizable kind. That means . . . but I don't think I have to tell you." Cups his ear, aims it at the moon, listens. "Or could be you speak so low I can't hear you. Or one has to make an appointment to speak with you since so many may want to. That it? Well of course you can't answer if it was: the necessary appointment first. You might not even be listening. But you'd have to be if one did have to make an appointment to speak to you, but forget it, all to most of that. To be safe: all." Thinks: Why am I talking so ridiculously? Moon making me do it: full, and calm face that makes me nervous, besides the heavenly night? From now on just look at the moon, forget talking to it, because you also might wake one of the family. Looks. Nice round face, round nice face, some cultures—no, don't start saying what some other cultures see in the configurations of the moon that we see as a face. Rabbits, monkeys; one culture, just the profile of a duck. But he told himself not to say. Just look, see what comes from that. Does. It's a nice sight, that's all. Meaning: that's plenty, maybe more than plenty, so what more can he say? Nice sight, nice round face, in ways there can be nothing more beautiful anywhere at any time than this kind of night with this kind of light. Bright, clear, full moon, stars, no other light but from that lighthouse five or so miles away, perfect weather so to speak, perfect night so to speak, every now and then bird sounds, loons, steady clicks and hum of harmless insects, no planes, no disturbances, no natural or man-made rumblings, beautiful view, everything perfect, so to speak, his health good, life with his wife very good, kids healthy and fine and sound asleep, rest of the world's what it is, but most of it now seems at peace. Things seem to be going relatively well almost everywhere right now, better in the universe that he knows than at any time he's known it. This is a great moment, these have been great minutes, everything near to being perfect as things can come near to being that, so to speak, mind alive, active, excited, enthusiastic, he feels good, he doesn't know how he could ever feel better, if he went to bed now and felt like sex he's sure no matter how tired his wife was she'd comply. But he could fall asleep with her or alone on that chaise longue there and it would feel as good. There are no threats, demands, regrets, nothing he wants, right now everything's right, what more could he want than this night, what more any other day or night could he want? So this is the end then. The end. This is it, so to speak. Can't think of anything else. Can't speak. Stares for a long time at the moon. Minutes. Tries to see if he can stare at it without anything coming into his head. Things come but nothing much. Feels so damn good, feels at peace. Then gets a little tired on his feet and with just staring at the moon and the moon seeming to stay in place and just about everything else around him seeming the same, and heads for the house, thinks should he stay out a few more minutes, a single minute, thirty seconds then to see if anything else comes into his head? Do. Does. Minutes, looks at the moon. Sits on the chaise longue. Nothing else comes. No other good thoughts, he means. And even more tired now, so goes inside, pees, not because he has to but so he doesn't have to get up later when he's much sleepier in bed, gets into bed, close to his wife, she's on her side, he feels—can't see much of her because the moon's on the other side of the house and doesn't give off much light on this one, so he'd want that, moon to be on this side shining through the window here, where he can see it and his wife on her side, his wife nude with the covers off and on her side, the curves that look like lots of things, hills, mountains, valleys, dunes, the moon and various phases of it, where he can wake up his wife and make love with her to moonlight, start to make love by moving his hands along the valleys and dunes and then make full love, from behind, below, the side, atop, where the moon's face can watch them, so to speak, where the moon can make love with them, so to speak, or rather take part in or contribute to that love-making in several ways he'll say, just that they know it's watching, so to speak, and they're doing it to its light. "Moon," he says, softly so she can't hear, "come to this side of the house so you can give us some light." Moon does. Suddenly it's there. There's no way anyone can describe the moon the way it is now—a bauble, a ball, a cheap ear pendant, a globe or lantern or round yellow squash or fruit, none of those work, moon's just there, all the light he needs. He wakes his wife by saying her name several times. She says "What?" Did it also by shaking her shoulder gently. He says "A miracle." She says "What?" He says "You asking what miracle or just what?" "What?" Back's to him, all those curves. He glides his hand over them and gets his mouth up to her exposed ear and says "I asked the moon to come to this side of the house so I could see it and see you and your body and everything and it did." "What moon? What side?" "The moon; there's only one; the moon." "Where, I mean? Why'd you wake me?" "To make love to you to moonlight." "That's nice," she says, "and you know me, always game," and moves her head around so they can kiss. After they do she looks past his face and says "I don't see any moon." "You don't?" He turns around—back's been to the window–and looks outside. He sees it, right out there, framed by the window, just the moon in a totally cloudless dark sky, how can't she see? "You don't see what I see?" he says. "If it's the moon you say you're seeing, no, I can't." "But it's there." "Where?" "Oh, well, I thought I had powers." "Let's go outside then if you want to make love by moonlight," she says. "That is what you want to do, right?" "With," he says, "but I'll take without. But we don't have a bed out there, and the grass will be wet and, even if we brought two or three blankets to lie on, they'd soon be soaked through." "The chaise longue, of course." "It's too narrow. One of us can barely lie on it straight." "We don't have to do it the same old way," she says. "It's warm here." "We'll be warm," she says, "don't worry. But if you don't want to, fine, but I'm ready. I thought you'd try while I was reading." "I was reading too and I didn't think you wanted to."

"Come," she says. She gets out of bed, grabs his hand. "Take a couple of blankets," she says. He takes them off the bed and goes outside with her. Moon's there, full, bright, little beard this time instead of a toupee. Beard disappears, and then it's just a beatific face again or what looks to him like one. "Sit," she says. He does, where she tells him to, at the end of the chaise longue. She sits on him, facing him. They do it this way. At the end they both howl. Moon disappears at almost that exact moment. "Clouds," he says after. "Shame," she says.

Stephen Dixon is the author of many books, including *Fourteen Stories, Time to Go,* and *All Gone* (all available from Johns Hopkins), as well as the acclaimed novel *Frog.* About three hundred of his short stories have appeared in journals, magazines, and anthologies. He has won two National Endowments for the Arts fellowships, three O. Henry Prizes, a Guggenheim Fellowship for fiction, and an American Academy and Institute of Arts and Letters Award in Literature. He teaches writing and literature at the Johns Hopkins University. *Long Made Short* is his tenth collection of short stories and contains two prizewinners: "The Rare Muscovite" (O. Henry Prize) and "Man, Woman, and Boy" (Best American Stories).

Fiction Titles in the Series

Guy Davenport, *Da Vinci's Bicycle: Ten Stories*

Stephen Dixon, *Fourteen Stories* ✓

Jack Matthews, *Dubious Persuasions*

Guy Davenport, *Tatlin!*

Joe Ashby Porter, *The Kentucky Stories*

Stephen Dixon, *Time to Go*

Jack Matthews, *Crazy Women*

Jean McGarry, *Airs of Providence*

Jack Matthews, *Ghostly Populations*

Jean McGarry, *The Very Rich Hours*

Steve Barthelme, *And He Tells the Little Horse the Whole Story*

Michael Martone, *Safety Patrol*

Jerry Klinkowitz, *"Short Season" and Other Stories*

James Boylan, *Remind Me to Murder You Later*

Frances Sherwood, *Everything You've Heard Is True*

Stephen Dixon, *All Gone: Eighteen Short Stories*

Jack Matthews, *Dirty Tricks*

Joe Ashby Porter, *Lithuania*

Robert Nichols, *In the Air*

Ellen Atkins, *World Like a Knife*

Greg Johnson, *A Friendly Deceit*

Jack Matthews, *"Storyhood As We Know It" and Other Stories*

Stephen Dixon, *Long Made Short*